Ellen Palmer Allerton

Annabel

And Other Poems

Ellen Palmer Allerton

Annabel
And Other Poems

ISBN/EAN: 9783744765381

Printed in Europe, USA, Canada, Australia, Japan

Cover: Foto ©Andreas Hilbeck / pixelio.de

More available books at **www.hansebooks.com**

AND

OTHER POEMS.

BY

ELLEN P. ALLERTON.

NEW YORK:
JOHN B. ALDEN, PUBLISHER.
1885.

PRINTING AND BOOKBINDING COMPANY,
NEW YORK.

INTRODUCTION.

MANY of the poems in this volume have been printed in the newspapers of the West; and the kindness accorded them by editors and readers has encouraged me to collect and preserve them in more enduring form. They are the work of such hours of leisure as a busy life on a farm has afforded me. In the green heart of the country, among rural sights and sounds, they have been conceived and written.

I send out my little book in hope and faith, trusting that its gospel of Work and of cheerful Content may find its way to many a quiet fireside. If it but serve to brighten homely toil with a touch of the ideal, and to beguile, now and then, a weary hour for the "tired mothers" of our land, its mission will have been accomplished.

ELLEN PALMER ALLERTON.

HAMLIN, BROWN CO., KANSAS, *May* 2, 1885.

CONTENTS.

ANNABEL.

A POEM OF THE HEART.

I.

Look there, my friend, through yonder clump
    of trees.
You see that lofty, weather-beaten wall?
You hear the hum of wheels, the broken fall
Of pent-up waters borne along the breeze?
That is the old brown mill. Its walls have
    stood
While children's children have grown old
    and gray,
While ruthless axes have hewn down the
    wood,
And yonder town has grown, rood after rood,
The mill has stood there as it stands to-day.

II.

You wonder why I point it out to you?
Well, listen. You shall hear a simple tale—
Simple in homely truth—which cannot fail
To wake your tender pity; which must sue
Your heart—you have a heart—to charity.
Only a story of a child's mistake;
Of blindness lifted when too late to see;
Of woman's waking when too late to wake;
Of man's strong passion hardly kept in
    check;
And the strange ending—if things end at
    all—
I sometimes fancy they do not, but break
    and break,
In ceaseless ripples, such as crimp the lake
When in its depths one lets a pebble fall.

III.

Come down the stream a little way, and look
Behind those drooping elms. You see
A low white cottage by the roaring brook,
With tangled garden, to its weeds forsook,
And broken panes, where rains beat dismally.
Almost within the shadows of the mill,
O'erhung and sheltered by yon craggy hill,
The cottage stands. And here, at eventide,
After a glorious, golden day of June,
John Dent, the miller, brought his girlish bride.

IV.

Across the valley had a marriage bell
Pealed joyfully at morn. A child had stood
(She was but little more)—young Annabel—
And uttered vows which only womanhood,
Full-grown and earnest, knowing well itself,
Should dare to utter. It was not for pelf--
No scheming child of sordid need was she—
But prone to meet true kindness gratefully,
As buds beneath the sunshine ope and lift.
And when young John had wooed her ten-
      derly,
And honestly, (an honest man was he)
She gave him—so she thought—her heart's
      best gift.

V.

Had she but lived and died and never known,
As many women do; had she not learned
What else she had to give—what slow fires
      burned,
Smouldered and hid, fed by themselves alone;
Had no hand stirred them to a quenchless
      blaze,
All had gone well—no, loveless is not well—
But had not gone so ill. Sad, sad to tell
How woke into a wail the silent tone;
How evil stole into her quiet days;
How throbbed her heart-strings like a funeral
      knell.

VI.

For years her life was calm. Sweetly she
    went
Calm household ways, and kept her hearth-
    stone bright.
Light was her heart at noon, serene at night,
In simple kindliness was well content.
Yet oft she wondered why the tenderness
That closely clasped her in its folding arm,
Could wake no passion-throb of happiness;
Why loving words, so earnest and so warm,
Should have so little potency to charm.
Chided herself, and blamed her girlish heart
Because it gave so little—so much less
Than what was given her—so kept apart,
And would not leap and thrill at love's
    caress.

VII.

And when her first-born laughed upon her
    knee,
And looked up with its father's honest eyes
Into her own, with innocent surprise,
She wondered why a baby's careless glee,
Its clasping fingers and its aimless kiss,
Should wake within her heart such throbbing
    bliss,
Where all before had been so calm and still.
Yet more she blamed herself—resolved to be
Indeed a loving wife henceforth. Ah me!
She had to learn that love comes not at will,
But grows—if grown at all—spontaneously;
Its clasping tendrils oft refuse to twine,
Nor unto careful pressure flows its wine.

VIII.

Thus ran the days: at morn her household
    toil,
Then needlework or books, both new and old;
And whatsoever poets sang or told
Found in her hungry heart a fertile soil.

The mighty masters' strains were household
    words,
So often had she conned them o'er and o'er;
And humbler poets' lays and songs of birds
Blended their music round her cottage door.
She trained her flowers, sang her cradle
    songs,
And taught her babe to lisp its father's name
First of all words; and softly went and came,
And neither talked nor thought of woman's
    wrongs.

IX.

In afternoons of sunny summer days,
Along the path that runs beside the hill—
Now overgrown with weeds—to yonder mill
She turned her feet; and where the sunlight
    plays
There in the doorway through those giant
    trees,
The child beside her, and the toying breeze
Lifting the ringlets of her dusky hair,
She sat, the while her husband plied his toil,
Oft noting, as he passed, the picture fair
Of child and mother—often pausing there
To touch her brow, or lift a ringlet's coil.

X.

So passed the days. The brook went down
    the glen
After its labor, singing on its way.
Like task-bound school-boy just let out to
    play;
The great trees rustled—there were many
    then—
As summer winds, flapping their lazy wings,
Came down among them from the breezy
    hill;
The vale was fresh and green with growing
    things;
And peace, such peace as only duty brings,
Sat there within the shadow of the mill.

XI.

Meanwhile the child-wife grew to woman-
hood,
Unfolding with her life but half complete,
Although she knew it not—her willing feet,
And hands as willing, doing naught but good.
And was she beautiful? 'Tis woman-like
To ask the question. Yes; yet none could
tell
Wherein her beauty lay. I could not strike
Her picture, had I all the thousand dyes
That paint the air. Dark were her eyes—
This I remember—with softly gleaming lights
Trembling within their depths, as in a well
You catch the sheen of stars on summer
nights.

XII.

You bid me hasten, and you wonder why
I do not tell my story and have done.
I pray your patience—'tis so sad a one,
I linger at its borders tremblingly.
But here it is: On one ill-fated morn, ·
A senseless form was laid beneath her roof,
Bleeding and bruised, with garments smeared
and torn,
And clotted hair, all red with ghastly gore.
"Here, Annabel!" said John, and said no
more;
He knew her tender heart—it was enough.

XIII.

Asking no questions, with her gentle hands
She washed the blood from the pale, swollen
face,
And from the matted hair, and sought apace
To win him back to life. The loosened bands
Tightened at last; the silent, pulseless wheel
Of life turned slowly round; he oped his
eyes—
Blue eyes they were—and looked with blank
surprise

On the kind faces bent beside the bed;
Asked where he was, and how he came to
feel
So bruised and battered—and what ailed his
head.
"We picked you up," said John, "by yonder"
cliff—
A broken limb, bruised head—if that is all.
I saw your horse take fright, and shy and
fall,
Wrenching a sapling from its rocky bed.
She fell beneath you—so did save your life,
We hope and trust — the noble beast is
dead."

XIV.

"Poor Nan!" the stranger sighed, "I loved
her well.
The graceful creature was my truest friend;
And I could weep that thus should be her
end.
What frighted her I'm sure I cannot tell.
She never once her foothold lost before,
And we have traversed half a continent.
I do remember that she shied—no more.
Poor Nan! Ah well! I ought to be content,
And bless the fates that brought me to your
door."

XV.

The surgeon came and set the broken limb,
And Annabel looked on with pitying eye
The while her tender tears fell silently,
And thought him brave—admired the cour-
age grim
That bore the wrench and strain unflinch-
ingly.
He never winced; the weakness of a groan
Parted not once the pallor of his lips.
So still he lay, but for clenched finger-tips,
You might have thought him senseless as a
stone.

XVI.

A woman's pity is a dangerous thing;—
Most when its softness is all mixed and blent
With woman's admiration. Such content
It hath of passion and of tenderness,
Which from its tearful dew luxuriant spring,
That she who feels needs double guardedness
O'er her heart's citadel; and all the more,
When in that heart lie mines of untold
    wealth
Unwrought by human hand. Its golden ore,
Unlocked, unguarded, yields to subtle stealth.

XVII.

For weeks the stranger lay, fevered and ill,
Tossing at times in wild delirium,
At others, lying faint and pale and dumb,
In limp exhaustion, without speech or will.
Oft in his fevered ravings he would talk
Of distant scenes—a spray-washed seaside
    home;
Of his young sisters—then he seemed to walk
By forest streams, or mountain passes clomb.
He raved of the Sierras; tossed a rock
Over the crags towards the Western Sea,
Marked its reboundings with a ghastly glee,
And laughed at each reverberating shock.

XVIII.

At last the fires burned out. Life seemed to
    stand
Poised on a balance. Breathless days he lay,
With his pale brow by chill, damp breezes
    fanned
From off another shore. Within the shad-
    ows dim
That fringe the skirts of that uncertain land
From whence no traveller o'er the misty rim
Comes with returning feet, day after day
He lingered at the borders, as if Death,
Putting his hot sword back into its sheath,
Having won fairly, scorned to take his prey.

XIX.

Meanwhile young Annabel, watching his
    lightest sigh,
With sleepless eyes above his pillow hung;
And when the folded portals backward
    swung,
And the ebbed tides came faintly flowing in,
She bowed her stately head, and silently—
So glad was she that life at last should win—
Wept tears of joy. Such tears are soonest dry!

XX.

Then came the days, so slow and yet so swift,
Of convalescence—days when vanquished
    pain
Flees back among the shadows—when again
The prostrate forces slowly, feebly lift,
Like the bowed spears of tempest-beaten grain.
Then Robert Lorne, with puzzled pleased sur-
    prise,
Did first discover what a lovely nurse
He had; marked—what I've told you in my
    verse—
Her dusky ringlets and her starry eyes;
And then he wondered, thought, and won-
    dered still,
What freak of fortune, what mistake of fate,
Had planted such a regal flower as that
Within the shadow of a dusty mill.

XXI.

Such thoughts were dangerous—like her pity.
    Time
Wore on, and as the sick man restless grew,
Impatient of his weakness, ('tis his due
To say, he had been patient in his pain)
She brought her books, and tried the sooth-
    ing chime
Of flowing measures and of tender rhyme;
And read to him, in cadence clear and sweet,
That seemed to him, in its low rhythmic beat,
Like the soft footfalls of the summer rain.

XXII.

They talked together, and he wondered more:
How had she gathered in that quiet vale,
Where pompous Learning ne'er had swept its
    trail,
Of wit and wisdom such a wondrous store?
He drew her on, and sounded hidden wells
That into sparkling streamlets bubbled o'er,
As pure, sweet springs that never flowed be-
    fore,
Start at a touch along the bosky dells.
Her inner life, its strange, sweet mysteries,
Lay all unrolled before his eager eyes—
So frankly talked she—to her own surprise—
And oft her laugh rang out, like tinkling
.   bells.

XXIII.

Sweet were those days, without a thought of
    wrong—
Days that on swift and gilded pinions sped—
Ere Conscience had tolled out her stern
    alarm,
And pointed to the rocks that loomed ahead.
Would that no other came into my song!
You see what baleful shadow, dire and dim,
Hovered about the sick-room, stole apace
Into the unbarred door, and held the place?
It came to this—he loved her, she loved him.

XXIV.

There came an hour when but a little thing—
A thoughtless act, and innocent, because
It held no guilty thought of broken laws—
Revealed it to them both. He was asleep—
At least she thought he was—the fanning
    wing
Of a stray breeze tossing the chestnut hair
That lay about his brow; and Annabel,
Rising to leave the room, just stooped her
    there,
2

Softly put back the clusters, softly laid ·
Her sweet warm cheek upon it. Then dis-
　　mayed,
She heard the voice of warning, knew it well.
She felt a thrill that never once before
Had stirred her heart—that never, never-
　　more
Must stir it thus again. Alas! the fate
That had withheld such sweetness till too
　　late!

XXV.

Then knew he that she loved him—raised his
　　arms,
And would have clasped her, but she turned,
While all her face with scorching blushes
　　burned,
And left him—with a thousand vague alarms
Tossing the heart, which, at that mute caress,
Had, for one moment, leaped with happiness.

XXVI.

Thenceforth her manner changed. She silent
　　grew,
And often met with an averted eye
His questioning look; and well and faithfully
Strove with her foe, determined to subdue.
Meanwhile the man grew strong. His hurts
　　were well,
And the soft tints of health began to come
Across the sunken pallor of his cheek.
He took slow walks—still further cure to
　　seek—
Adown the brook, and through the grassy
　　dell,
And soon began to speak of going home.

XXVII.

" 'Tis a long journey," said the miller, "wait
Awhile; be not in haste to go, I pray.
You had best tarry, and submit to fate,"
Laughed he, " 'till you have strength enough
　　to shut the gate—

(He just had left it wide) you've not, to-day."
Poor man! he little knew what meaning fell
From out his careless banter, on the ears
Of guest and wife. No truant, tell-tale tears
Sprang to her eyes; she kept her bosom's
strife
On its own battle-field, and marshalled well
Her gathered forces, even while a knell,
Struck on her heartstrings, sent its hollow
toll
In sobbing shudders through her inmost
soul.
There lay her dead—a scathed and blighted
life.

XXVIII.

"If go you must," said honest John, "good-
by.
The mill awaits me with its silent wheels;
The summer morn with quiet footstep steals
Quickly away, and so, perforce, must I."—
"Farewell," said Robert Lorne. "My thanks
accept
For all your kindness. I shall hold it well,
With grateful care, among my treasures
kept."
"Small thanks to me," said John. "The
praise is due,
To yonder tireless nurse who tended you.
With her I leave you—talk to Annabel."

XXIX.

So briskly towards the mill he walked away,
Humming a tune in careless, happy tone,
Leaving the two, and so they stood alone.
What could they do? and what could either
say?
Only good-by? Had they but said no more,
Love might have died a silent, smothered
death,
Like fires close-covered where there stirs no
breath.

But words are flame; once given vent and
    space,
The fiery tide fast over leaps its shore,
And seldom ebbs again into its place.

XXX.

One silent moment—save the throbbing beat
.With which two hearts kept time—and then
    he came
And stood beside her, trembling. "I can
    tame,"
Said he, "the wild mustang, though strong
    and fleet,
But cannot tame my heart. Turn not away
That sad, pale face. Hear me this once, I
    pray,
For I must speak or die—though years too
    late.
John Dent spoke truly, though he little
    knew
How what he said was doubly, direly true;
I have *not* strength enough to shut the gate.

XXXI.

"I know you love me—nay, hide not your
    face,
Drop not your eye—'tis veiled e'en now with
    tears.
Let me look deep into its starry glow
Once more—it is the last, last time, you
    know.
I knew you loved me, when, with tender
    grace,
You stooped and touched me with your
    cheek. The years,
Many or few, that slowly come and go,
One thing cannot take with them. I shall
    keep,
Hidden within my lone heart's deepest deep,
The memory of one moment's happiness,
When throbbed my whole soul to that mute
    caress."

XXXII.

"You should not say such things to me!"
    she said.
Entreaty and reproach were in her look;
Her face was deadly pale, her whole frame
    shook.
"You see my weakness, which I seek to
    tread,
With all my gathered strength, beneath my
    feet;
The task is hard enough—why will you add
Strength to my enemy and steal my own?
Leave me, I pray, and let me fight alone
The weary battle—I am sick and sad."

XXXIII.

"Poor little one!" he said. "I pity you
From my heart's core, but do myself as well.
How it shall fare with me I cannot tell;
But you will be to every duty true,
And go your daily ways like some sweet
    saint,
With feet that never falter, though you
    faint.
You, but a frail woman, will a foe subdue
That conquers me—I cannot be like you."

XXXIV.

"'Tis only to endure," she said. "The pain,
Though sharp, will soon be over. We must
    take
The sequence of our folly. They that make,
As we have made, shipwreck of happiness,
Must fare without it. Life is not so long—
What signifies a heartache more or less?
A few wild throbs that wrench the breast and
    brain,
Then—if we conquer—comes the calm of
    peace;
Next, that of Death, and then—all struggles
    cease."

XXXV.

"'Tis a sad end that only comes with death!
I think the saddest thing that mortals know
Is such a love, that only endeth so.
O Annabel! down to my latest breath
Must I endure this wrong—'the perfect mate
After long years of waiting found too late'?
Matches, they say, are made in Heaven above,
Where hearts are wed. If marriage is but
    love,
All other marriage, then, must spurious be,
And you, before high Heaven, belong to me."

XXXVI.

"Forbear!" the woman cried. "'Twas hard
    before:
'Tis cruel that you add such agony,
Heaping it high upon my misery.
Oh! cease, and leave me—I can bear no
    more."
"I go: but once, just once, your heart shall
    throb—
Where it should always throb—close up to
    mine."
He clasped her close, and while sob after sob
Shook her from head to foot, on brow and
    neck,
On tear-wet cheek, and pale and quivering lip,
Pressed passionate kisses. Little did he reck
In that mad moment of the bitter drip
So sure to follow that one draught of wine.

XXXVII.

You blame such madness? so do I, but then
Poor human nature, wrenched and passion-
    tossed,
At best intent too often goes astray.
We little know how much our own, so crossed,
Could bear—whether the strength, which in
    our day
Of sunny peace deems so secure, could stand
Amid the sweeping storm, and hold at bay

The rush of passion, stem the tide of pain,
And probe our own deep wounds with steady
　hand.
We know not until tried, I say again,
What we can bear.　We all have need to pray.

XXXVIII.

At last he whispered hoarsely, "Fare thee
　well.
Earth holds no parting half so sad as this.
Would it had been but death! no tolling bell
Did ever utter forth such wretchedness.
You will find peace—such peace as waits to
　bless
Enduring patience; but, oh Annabel!
Sometimes when, in your saintly purity,
At the still evening hour you kneel to pray,
Remember and ask pity, too, for me."
He loosed his arms, then turned and rushed
　away.
She stood and watched him from the open
　door—
Once stretched her hands ('twas well he did
　not see)
As if to call him back—cried, "Woe is me!
I never, never shall behold him more!"
Then she caught up her boy, and held him
　prest,
While she wept wildly, to her aching breast.
　　*　　*　　*　　*　　*　　*　　*　　*

XXXIX.

A year had flown on slow and quiet wing
Above the vine-wreathed cottage by the mill.
Again the wild rose all along the hill
Hung out its lavish blossoms.　All the ground
Was spread with summer's richness: on the
　wing
The wild bird sang—and still the wheels went
　round.
It was a fragrant morning; every breath of
　air

Was laden with the breezy scents of June.
From out the open casement a low tune
Came softly floating, like a tender prayer—
The wife was singing at her daily care.
Just shadowed was her brow with pensive
    thoughts,
Yet was it calm and smooth and purely fair—
'Twas plain had come to her the peace she
    sought.

XL.

But how fared Robert Lorne? Not quite so
    well.
With restless foot, that never ceased to roam,
He wandered widely, and no chosen home
Found anywhere. The ocean's heaving swell
Best suited him; and mountain heights
Swept by wild tempests; stormy nights,
When shook and jarred the everlasting hills
Beneath the tread of thunders, when the glare
Of the red lightnings lit the midnight air,
And sweeping torrents tore the mountain
    side—
These chimed with his dark mood. But peace-
    ful vales,
And silent rivers with their gentle glide,
And sleeping lakes flecked with the snowy sails
Of floating ships; the calm of eventide,—
All scenes of quiet—in his feverish soul
But stirred the demon of unrest. The bowl
Of fierce excitement, with a restless thirst
Deeply he quaffed, yet still, as at the first,
He thirsted. At last, heart-sick and sore,
When utter weariness had done its worst,
He turned his face toward his native shore.

XLI.

"Once more," he thought, "to look upon her
    face,
Unseen by her. I will not break the calm
Which she, mayhap, hath found. Her tender
    palm

She need not lift to warn me from the place.
But once to watch her in her gentle grace,
Twining, perchance, the roses at her door.
It shall be only once—I'll dare no more."

XLII.

And so it chanced, that breezy morn of June, [hill,
Crouching within the copse that crowned the
He listened to the low and pensive tune
That floated through the casement. Waiting still,
He saw not though he heard her. Finally
She came within the doorway—raised her hand
To shade her eyes, and with a startled look
Gazed down the beaten pathway by the brook.
He wondered at her air. What did she see?
Following her eye with his, he saw a man
With wild, excited mien, and hurried tread,
Approach to where she stood—heard what he said:
"Your husband, madam! Quickly as you can
Come to the mill. He's hurt, and well-nigh dead."

XLIII.

Swiftly she flew, as if her feet had wings,
To where he lay. He saw, looked up and smiled.
Whispered, "Good-by—God keep my wife and child!"
Then closed his eyes upon all earthly things.
Now swept across her soul a grief so wild
That reason nearly reeled. Regret, remorse,
Uttered accusing voices. Had she been
Within her secret heart a loyal wife,
She had not felt the pain, so swift and keen,
That cut her conscience like a two-edged knife.

The sight, the sound, were pitiful! A low moan
Came from the set white lips; no tears she
  shed,
But gazed with stony look upon the dead.
At last a voice, in low and husky tone:
"Take her away. Do you not see," it said,
"That this is killing her?" She raised her eyes
With one quick glance of sudden, shocked
  surprise,
Saw it was He, and fainted on the corse.

XLIV.

He came not near her in her grief, but when
The day of burial came, he watched afar,
With strange emotions in his heart at war.
He saw her, sable-clad and drooping, stand
Beside the open grave, clasping the hand
Of her half-orphaned boy. and pitied her—
So sad, so drooping did she seem—and then
There crossed his pity a wild wave of joy,
(Albeit remorse came in with its alloy)
That, howsoever stricken, she was free.
"Sure none may claim her now," he thought,
  "but me."

XLV.

A month went by, and then a letter came,
Telling her that when the year was done,
Its last day faded, its last setting sun
Gone out of sight with all its hues of flame,
She might expect him at her cottage door.
"Fail not," it said, " to look for me at even;
If living, you will see me—not before.
I well can wait a year without complaint,
With hope to lighten with its joyous leaven—
I who did think to wait forevermore.
Though love is haste, it still hath self-re-
  straint;
And not a slander, not a breath of taint,
Must soil the white plumes of my bird of
  heaven."
*   *   *   *   *   *

XLVI.

The year at last had fled.   The scents of June
Once more went floating softly down the dell;
Once more the tall grass rocked beneath the
    swell
Of summer winds; in noisy, babbling rune
The brook came singing from the creaking
    mill;
And once again, along the beetling hill
The wild rose hung its pennons.   Evening
    fell;
The sunset faded, and the summer moon
Rose calmly, and hung out her silver shield
Athwart the dusky bosom of the night.
One star, and then another, in the field
Of heaven came out and blossomed into light.
Silence unbroken hung about the door
Of the lone cottage, only o'er and o'er
From out the shadows one sad whip-po-will
Sang his night-song, so plaintive, yet so shrill,
And the brook babbled to its sedgy shore.

XLVII.

Within sits Annabel, and counts the ticks
That measure off the travel step by step,
Of the slow, laggard Time.   In rosy sleep
Her play-tired darling lies.   A silence deep—
The silence of hushed waiting—wraps her
    round.
She listens for a footstep, for a sound beside.
Both come at last.   The low gate clicks;
Upon the gravelled walk a manly tread,
Firm, eager, then, a quick rap at the door;
Then, "Robert!" "Annabel!" and then no
    more
In those first moments is by either said.
What need of words?   Her head is on his
    breast,
His arms about her, and both hearts at rest.
What need, when each knew all that each
    could say?

Thus, deep emotion, with its fetters flung
About the speech, hath oft "tied fast the
　　tongue."
Love, like a brook, starts singing on its way,
Ripples and murmurs in its noisy play;
Like a deep river when it meets the sea,
It rolls into its ocean silently.

XLVIII.

Again the wedding bells, above the town
And through the valley, where a year ago
Sobbed forth a funeral knell so sad and slow,
Pealed out in throbs of joy. Love wore its
　　crown
In solemn awe; for well did those two know
How in its hunger it had wronged the dead.
Yet both had sought to quench it; both had
　　tried
To kill a deathless thing—which had not died.
Their joy was born of sorrow. Solemnly
They held in close embrace their child of
　　tears.
The bride is pale, though lovely. Shadows
　　lie
Within her glorious eyes; she trembles, fears;
Amid her joy half shivers as with dread;
And yet the words she utters now are true.
It is her heart that speaks—this time she
　　knew
The full, sweet meaning of the words she
　　said.

XLIX.

They went away; and in far foreign lands,
Through Old World scenes they wandered at
　　their will.
They heard no more the clatter of the mill,
Although the busy sounds did never cease;
Although still turned the tireless wheels and
　　bands;
The walls still throbbed and trembled; and
　　within

Beat ceaseless pulses, sounded ceaseless din.
Did they come back again? You soon shall
    know.
I have not told you all the story yet;—
Would I could leave it here, the rest forget!

L.

At last the lovers—(they were lovers still,
As when they stood together, groom and
  · bride)—
Weary of travel, longed to sit at peace
In their own doorway; dreamed of winter
    nights
With talk or books by their own chimney-
    side,
While on the panes should beat the whirling
    snow;
Of children's play, and all home's dear de-
    lights.
And so they sought a vessel homeward bound,
And rode once more upon the summer sea.
One precious treasure they abroad had found,
And Annabel was full of happy care—
She held a baby girl upon her knee,
Born at the foot of Alps, on storied ground.
Her boy played round her in his sturdy
    glee,
While sweet sea-breezes tossed his flaxen
    hair;
Her husband lingered near with ready aid
(In truth, one seldom found him otherwhere);
And hardy sailors, brown with ocean toil,—
Profane, perhaps, for life before the mast
Is rough, we know,—full oft their footsteps
    staid
For lingering, softened glances as they passed,
Thinking of what they nevermore might see—
Of wife and babes, and home, and native soil.
Swift flew the hours. None saw the spectre
    gray
That hovered near and nearer day by day.

LI.

A night, a moonlit night upon the deep.
A night of breathless calm; a night so still,
The circling waste of waters lay asleep,
And one scarce felt the ocean's pulses thrill.
A night to dream upon in after years,
On shaded porch, by cheerful ingle-nook,
Or in hot rooms, beside the singing brook—
'Twas surely not a night for groans and tears.

LII.

The children slept below; and Annabel,
Robert, and others stood about the deck,
Watching a ship that seemed a distant speck
Across the moon's white wake; enjoying well,
As only landsmen can, a calm at sea.
A little cry—"Oh, Robert! what is that?
That beauty down there?" "That's a shark,"
   said he.
"A big one, too, he is, and plump and fat,—
But hungry now, and watching for a feast.
What jaws, and teeth! ugh! 'tis an ugly
   beast!"
Just then, as some one spoke, he turned away,
Not thinking how one moment's heedlessness
A man may rue until his dying day.
There lay the monster, silent, motionless,
With wicked, watchful eyes, and gleaming
   breast
Half upturned to the moon; and Annabel
Gazed as one charmed. She shuddered and
   turned pale,
Yet with dilated eyes leaned o'er the rail.
Farther she leaned—too far—and slipped—
   and fell.

LIII.

I pass it o'er—that awful scene at sea—
The woman's shriek, the man's hoarse, dreadful cry;
The kind hands (were they kind?) holding by
   force

The frantic husband in his agony
(To leap had been but death, to live was
    worse);
The shocked and pallid faces, horror-white;
And over all the calm moon's placid light.
Some things transcend the telling. Better
    these,
Left to that inner sense which hears and
    sees.

   *   *   *   *   *   *

LIV.

He still lives on, that sorely stricken man,
Lives, as man will, as even woman can,
When life no more holds any hope or joy.
He still is young—at least, is young in years—
Yet is the seal of age upon his brow.
The proud head droops, the kingly step is
    slow;
And round the temples, where the chestnut
    hair
Clustered in glassy sheen, cling locks of snow.
He comes here now and then—the sturdy
    boy,
The tiny dark-eyed girl beside him led—
The boy, like John Dent, open-browed and
    fair;
She, like her mother, with soft, dusky hair
Clinging in rings about her dainty head.
Eyes soft with pity mark them as they pass.
The children chatter—they are merry dears—
Proud when they win their father's smile.
    Alas!
His smile is sadder than a woman's tears.
The mill grinds on; the faithful wheels and
    bands
Take up their work each morn. The cottage
    stands
Untenanted, dismantled; no one heeds
The smothered flowers that choke amid the
    weeds.

I've seen the master pause—with shaking
    hands—
And close the gate. I think he dreads the
    spot.
My story ends. A strange one, is it not?

LV.

The twilight falls. The moon hangs o'er the
    hill;
The brook goes darkly down its winding way;
Ceased for the day the clatter of the mill;
Adown the valley stretch the shadows gray;
And you, I see, are weeping. Come away.

MISCELLANEOUS POEMS.

MY AMBITION.

I have my own ambition.   It is not
  To mount on eagle wings and soar away
Beyond the palings of the common lot,
  Scorning the griefs and joys of every day;
I would be human—toiling, like the rest,
With tender human heart-beats in my breast.

Not on cold, lonely heights, above the ken
  Of common mortals would I build my fame,
But in the kindly hearts of living men.
  There, if permitted, would I write my name;
Who builds above the clouds must dwell alone;
I count good fellowship above a throne.

And so, beside my door I sit and sing
  My simple strains—now sad, now light and gay;
Happy, if this or that but wake one string,
  Whose low, sweet echoes give me back the lay.
And happier still, if girded by my song,
Some strained and tempted soul stands firm and strong.

Humanity is much the same; if I
  Can give my neighbor's pent-up thought a tongue,
And can give voice to his unspoken cry
  Of bitter pain, when my own heart is wrung,—
Then we two meet upon a common land,
And henceforth stand together, hand in hand.

I send my thought its kindred thought to greet,
  Out to the far frontier, through crowded town.
Friendship is precious, sympathy is sweet;
  So these be mine, I ask no laurel-crown.
Such my ambition, which I here unfold;
So it be granted—mine is wealth untold.

MISCELLANEOUS POEMS.

A KANSAS PRAIRIE AND ITS PEOPLE.

How grandly vast the prairie seems,
  Beneath pale winter's glow—
A wide, white world, in death-like sleep
  Under its shroud of snow.

Yet there are signs of life; the lanes
  Are trod by heavy teams;
A horseman, on yon distant swell,
  A moving atom seems.

The wide, white lands that stretch away
  Are dotted everywhere
With orchard clumps, and farmers' homes
  Are snugly nestled there.

The people of this brave new world
  Have come from every quarter;
Some faced each other long ago,
  On red fields bathed in slaughter.

In frosty dawns of winter morns,
  The white smoke curls away
From homes of men who wore the blue,
  And men who wore the gray.

Here, brothers all, they hang their gifts
  On the same Christmas tree,
Are kindly neighbors, cordial friends,
  As brothers ought to be.

And crowds of children, Kansas born,—
  Our young State's hope and pride—
With rosy cheeks and sparkling eyes,
  Learn lessons side by side.

Naught reck they of the battle-field,
  Of sad, dark years of slaughter;
The Northman's son some day shall wed
  The Southron's gentle daughter.

WALLS OF CORN.

SMILING and beautiful, heaven's dome,
Bends softly over our prairie home,

But the wide, wide lands that stretched away,
Before my eyes in the days of May,

The rolling prairies billowy swell,
Breezy upland and the timbered dell,

Stately mansion and hut forlorn,
All are hidden by walls of corn.

All wide the world is narrowed down,
To walls of corn, now sere and brown.

What do they hold—these walls of corn,
Whose banners toss on the breeze of morn ?

He who questions may soon be told,
A great state's wealth these walls enfold.

No sentinels guard these walls of corn,
Never is sounded the warder's horn.

Yet the pillars are hung with gleaming gold,
Left all unbarred, though thieves are bold.

Clothes and food for the toiling poor,
Wealth to heap at the rich man's door;

Meat for the healthy, and balm for him
Who moans and tosses in chamber dim;

Shoes for the barefooted, pearls to twine
In the scented tresses of ladies fine;

Things of use for the lowly cot,
Where (bless the corn) want cometh not;

Luxuries rare for the mansion grand,
Gifts of a rich and fertile land;

All these things, and so many more
It would fill a book to name them o'er,

Are hid and held in these walls of corn,
Whose banners toss on the breeze of morn.

Where do they stand, these walls of corn,
Whose banners toss on the breeze of morn ?

Open the Atlas, conned by rule,
In the olden days of the district school.

Point to the rich and bounteous land,
That yields such fruits to the toiler's hand.

" Treeless desert," they called it then,
Haunted by beasts and forsook by men.

Little they knew what wealth untold,
Lay hid where the desolate prairies rolled.

Who would have dared, with brush or pen,
As this land is now, to paint it then ?

And how would the wise ones have laughed
    in scorn,
Had prophet foretold these walls of corn,
Whose banners toss in the breeze of morn ?

A HOME OUT WEST.

I.

A " PRAIRIE SCHOONER," creeping slow;
  A way-worn, jaded household band,
In eager voices, speaking low—
  Thus enter we the "promised land."
Behind us now the river's tide
Rolls dark and murky, deep and wide.

   *   *   *   *   *   *

II.

A warm May day; a sweet soft rain
  On a green prairie falling fast;
A stopping of the creeping wain,
  And the glad cry, "We're home at last."
After long weeks of travel sore,
The goal is won; we ask no more.

Home! with our roof the dripping sky,
  Our floor the rain-soaked prairie's breast!
Through all the wastes that round us lie,
  In wild, luxuriant verdure drest,
No tree extends its friendly bough,
We see no track of spade or plough.

   *   *   *   *   *   *

III.

A year has fled.   What wondrous change
  Has passed this way?   What sorcery,
What silent magic, swift and strange,
  Has wrought such wonders?   Come and
    see!
Where are the green wastes, soaked with
    rain?
You seek them?   You shall seek in vain.

Spring smiles again; the sunbeams play
  On gabled roof and crystal pane.
Spring smiles again; and skies of May
  Bend o'er broad fields of waving grain.

Here are young orchards; and the breeze
Bends the lithe limbs of forest trees.

The spring rains beat on snowy walls,
  Comely, though plain, snug-built and
    strong;
Through vine-wreathed windows sunshine
    falls,
  With cheerful smile, the whole day long;
And happy faces, fresh and bright,
Are gathered round the lamps at night.

Our prairie home is sweet and dear;
  The deep, rich soil holds honest wealth;
The airs we breathe are pure and clear;
  The free, strong winds waft life and health.
Here dwells Content from day to day;
So—let the great world go its way.

ON THE PRAIRIE.

OUT on the prairie—a shrieking storm!
  How the pitiless cold,
Driven from homes and firesides warm,
  In its terrible hold,
Here grapples and gripes with strength un-
    told!

Miles and miles, and nothing in sight,
  Only sweeps of snow—
That under the dusk of the gathering night,
  Now dimmer grow—
Breasting the winds, that fiercely blow.

Not a friendly light, not a sheltering tree,
  On the prairie's breast,
And my failing feet sink under me!
  I am heavy—oppressed
With a drowsy weight; I must stop and rest.

No, I cannot go on!   Here I lay me down,
    While the storm sweeps by;
Press on, if you can, to the sheltering town;
    In peace let me lie.
I am not cold—only sleepy—good-by.

———————

A LESSON FOR THE NEW YEAR.

THE last night of the year, I sat alone
    Beside the dying fire. The whole house
    slept.
Naught stirred the silence, save the wind's
    low moan,
    As sadly through the naked trees it crept,
The fall of embers and the clock's low beat,
That marked the passing year's retiring feet.

I was aweary; and the coming year
    Seemed but an added load that pressed me
    sore.
The morrow would bring friends, and I should
    hear
    The tread of many feet upon the floor.
I longed for quiet; I was vexed with care;
Just then my burden seemed too great to bear.

I thought of my unopened books, my pen,
    Lying long idle, rusting in its place.
Could I but take them to some lonely glen
    Where toil were not, nor any human face!
" 'Twere joy," cried I, so fretful was my mood
" To dwell one year in utter solitude."

" Have then thy wish! " was uttered sad and
    low;
    I turned, and One stood by me, fair and
    tall,
And from his countenance with light aglow,
    A look of pitying grief did on me fall.

"Have then thy wish!" He stooped and
  touched mine eyes,
And I stood dumb, overwhelmed with strange
  surprise.

The silent room had vanished, and a wood,
  Peopled with birds, that filled its aisles with
  song,
Compassed me round with sweet green soli-
  tude;
  A clear stream trailed its silver thread
  along;
And close beside it stood a rustic cot,
Piled high with volumes, and here toil was
  not.

Fruits for my food fell lightly at my feet;
  I was alone; through all that lovely place
I knew that I might wander, and not meet,
  In hill or hollow, any human face.
Within my books, all wit and wisdom blent.
I had my wish; was I therewith content?

Nay, verily. A sharp grief pierced me
  through,
  My spirit sank, oppressed with midnight
  gloom,
While trees hung o'er me, wet with heaven's
  dew.
  I felt as one walled up within a tomb.
I sought my books; locked were their stores
  from me;
The hot tears dimmed my sight, I could not
  see.

I tried my pen—in vain. No words would
  come.
  Thought was an arid desert, wide and gray,
From which no streams would flow. My soul
  was dumb
  With utter loneliness; but could I pray?

I cast me on the fragrant, dewy sod,
My face pressed in the grass—and cried to
  God.

"Oh! give me back," I prayed, "the dear
  days gone—
The toilsome days, so full of crowded care—
The hands I clasped, the lips that kissed my
  own.
  For these, for these, could I all burdens
    bear!"
I started, for a rustling robe trailed near;
And "Have again thy wish!" fell on my ear.

Again I felt soft, gentle fingers press
  Mine eyelids down; and lo! the dear old
    room,
The smiling lamplight, home's blest homli-
  ness!
  The lonely wood was gone, its grief, its
    gloom;
And close within my call my dear ones slept.
For very joy I bowed my head and wept.

The fire was dead, the moon shone on the
  snow,
  The wailing wintry wind blew bitter cold,
And yet I laid me down with heart aglow,
  For all life's leaden care seemed turned to
    gold.
I slept the sleep of peace; I rose at morn,
Strong in the glad New Year—as one new-
  born.

GENTLE SPRING.

These are signs of gentle Spring:
Flocks of wild geese on the wing,
Flying in a broken string:

Brooks that tumble, roar and rush,
Sinking drifts, and piles of slush,
And a universal mush.

Woman with a draggled dress,
Puddles that seem bottomless,
Roads all ditto—such a mess!

Horses flounder, loaded down;
Swearing driver—been to town
Curses, plunges—overthrown!

Fancy sleighs for sale at cost,
Balmy breezes, nipping frost,
Wild March mornings, tempest-tost.

Robins, blue-birds, sleet and snow,
Icy winds, and sunny glow—
What comes next you never know.

Sounds of coughs and choking wheezes,
And of loud, spasmodic sneezes,
Mingle with the straying breezes.

Handkerchiefs are bought and sold
By the dozen, I am told.
Question—" Have you had your cold?"

Come, ye singers, rise and sing!
Poets, tune your every string
For an ode to Gentle Spring.

A TRAIL OF "'49."

ACROSS the prairie where I dwell,
Stretches away, from swell to swell,
A road that might a story tell.

The track is wide and deeply cut
By wheels of heavy wagons, but
The rank grass grows in seam and rut.

'Tis the old trail of "Forty-nine";—
Thus history, in graven line,
Has stamped this prairie home of mine.

The years have passed, with snow and rain,
And mighty frosts upheaved—in vain—
For still this track shows clear and plain.

Tracing it where it winds away,
There comes to me, at twilight gray,
A vision of another day.

I see the covered wagons go,
Across the prairie toiling slow,
Through dreary storm, through summer glow.

I see them, with their human freight—
Hearts throbbing high with hope elate—
Pass onward to a doubtful fate.

Months pass; a weary, jaded train,
Worn with fatigue, disease and pain,
Creeps slowly o'er a desert plain.

Above, a cloudless, burning sky;
Below, naught greets the weary eye,
Save wastes of sand and alkali.

No rains descend, no water flows;
No cool trees bend, no green thing grows;
Yet still that sad train onward goes.

Fatigue and thirst! no tongue can tell
The victim's anguish, fierce and fell—
His fondest dream a bubbling well.

And some go mad and wildly rave;
Some find what, at the last, they crave,
The silence of a desert grave.

The living speak in husky tones;
The poor brutes drop with piteous moans;
The track is paved with bleaching bones.

Still onward—slower and more slow—
Dogged nightly by a stealthy foe,
Toward mountain passes choked with snow.

One sleeps, to dream of home and wife;
He wakes, at call to midnight strife
With tomahawk and scalping-knife.

 * * * * * * * *

Past perils, miseries untold,
Past desert heat, past mountain cold,
What waits them in the Land of Gold?

Go, search a checkered history
Of soon-got hoards, as soon to flee,
Of princely wealth and poverty.

Dark tales of crime, of murders fell,
Of drunken brawl, of gambling hell—
Good chroniclers have told them well.

Go, search them all, through every line—
Yet deign to read this song of mine,
Of the old trail of "Forty-nine."

A WAYSIDE TREE.

I PASSED to-day through a forest
 In soberest sombre drest;
Furled were the blood-red banners,
 Quenched was each flaming crest.

The wind swept through the branches;
 The clouds hung low and gray,
Bearing storms in their bosoms,
 Stealing the sun away.

The roar far back in the forest,
 The crackling above my head,
As the crisp leaves shook and shivered,
 Filled me with nameless dread.

Like the leaves, I shook and shivered
  As the cold wind colder blew,
And the tread of advancing tempests
  Sounded the deep woods through.

Was there nothing left of the summer ?
  Naught of the autumn show?
Nothing bright for the winter
  To fold in its sheets of snow?

Behold! by the dreary roadside,
  Towering fair and green
In the midst of its sombre sisters,
  A single oak is seen.

Touched with spatters of crimson,
  Bordered with fiery bands,
Across its resplendent garments
  The sun and the frost clasp hands.

I looked at the tree in wonder!
  It seemed like some ancient sage,
Wearing his youthful freshness
  Along with the frosts of age.

Oh! the life must be pure and noble
  That can keep, as the seasons go,
Its June and its rich October
  Till falleth the winter snow!

THE OLD BUTTERNUT TREE.

It stood by the old front gate—oh, long
    ago!—
Braving the summer storm and the winter
    snow;
And fresh among memory's treasures, so
  ' dear to me,
Stands in perpetual greenness that ancient
    tree.

Out on the roadside green, where passing feet
Turned to its wide-spread shade from the
  dusty street,
And laughing children, loitering home from
  school,
Sought, with their cheeks aflame, its shadows
  cool.

Here gathered the early birds, and built and
  sung;
The oriole's cunning nest from the branches
  swung;
Its broad arms sheltered from the noontide
  blaze;
And the nuts dropped on the turf in the autumn days.

In summer eves, when work was laid away,
And rest and coolness ended the sultry day,
When up the west the sunset unrolled its
  gold,
Like billows of gorgeous sea, fold over fold;

Then gathered the household band about the
  knee
Of the old butternut, the homestead tree.
They watched till the glow went out and dews
  came down,
And the moon wore up the east her silver
  crown.

All were together then; where are they now?
The world is wide, as sundered dear ones
  know;
And children, cradled on one mother's breast,
Scatter, like eaglets from their mountain
  nest.

The brothers are bearded men, and threads
  of gray
Whiten the clustering locks from day to day.

Each lights his household fire—so must it
    be—
While strangers sit in the shade of the dear
    old tree.

But, one sleeps on the hill, one far away,
And the gray-haired sire has lain, this many
    a day,
By the side of the mother who sang sweet
    lullabies,
And followed our childish feet with her gen-
    tle eyes.

A generation has passed and been laid away;
But the dear old roadside tree stands there
    to-day;
Hoary, and lopped, and scarred by many a
    storm,
Yet the summers still veil with leaves its bat-
    tered form.

Still stream through the broken boughs the
    sunset rays;
Still drop the nuts on the turf in the autumn
    days;
But the olden joys can never come back to
    me,
And the household gods have flown the home-
    stead tree.

TAUGHT BY A BIRD.

An April day: the cold wind blew,
The dark clouds lowered, the thick snow flew,
And where the springing grass lay green,
Ragged patches of white were seen.

Snow everywhere! I gazed with a sigh,
As the big flakes fell from the gloomy sky;

Loading the limbs of the budding trees,
Filling the hollows about their knees.

Had Winter come back—the vanquished
  king—
And rudely throttled the maiden, Spring?
But lo! from amid the storm I heard
The sweet, glad song of a tiny bird.

On a tufted twig, its feet in the snow,
Swung by the cold wind to and fro,
It sat and sang—that wee brown bird—
Putting to shame my petulant word.

The darkness lifted, the storm was done;
Through broken cloud-rifts shone the sun;
A breath came up from the south, and the
  snow
Melted away in the genial glow.

Spring reigned again; and again I heard
The joyous song of that dear brown bird.
With quickened pulses, and heart aglow,
I caught the refrain, "I told you so!"

Ah, little bird, had I faith like you,
When life and the world are dark to view!
When lowering skies are above me bent,
Could I feel your trust and your sweet con-
  tent!

You sang—your tender feet in the snow,
Swung by the cold wind to and fro.
Your faith was sure, and I now repeat
Over and over the lesson sweet.

THEN AND NOW.

BLEAK, rugged hills, o'er which the winter
  snow
    In wild gusts swept;
A sweet green vale, a calm lake, lying low,

Where osiers dipt;
A clear, cold spring, whose trickling overflow
Through tall grass crept.

There were some hearts that loved me. Till
my own
Shall cease to beat,
Whether I tread smooth ways, or jagged
stone
With bleeding feet,
I still shall hold them precious. (Love alone
Can make life sweet.)

Long years have fled. Still stand, deep scar-
red and hoar,
The wind-swept heights;
Still flows the spring, where parched lips,
thirsting sore,
Quaff deep delights;
Still sleeps the lake, by moonbeams silvered
o'er
On summer nights.

All these remain; scarce changed the peace-
ful scene,
Yet men grow old.
Locks that were dark are touched with frosty
sheen;—
Have hearts grown cold?
To know some few have kept the old love
green—
'Twere joy untold.

THE OLD FARMHOUSE.

A CRYSTAL spring, a sunny hill,
A gray old house with mossy sill,
Hemmed in by orchard trees,
With massive trunks and age untold,
Whose luscious fruits, like mounds of gold
When autumn nights grow crisp and cold,
Lay heaped about their knees.

And when the trees, bare, gaunt and grim,
Tossing aloft each naked limb,
   Breasted the sleety rain;
When summer sounds were heard no more,
When birds had sought a Southern shore,
When flowers lay dead about the door,
   And winter reigned again:

Then met the household band beside
A clean-swept hearth, a chimney wide,
   Where roared a maple fire.
When all the streams were fettered fast,
When fiercely blew the wintry blast,
And clouds of snow went whirling past,
   The logs were piled the higher.

How fondly memory recalls
The cheer within those old gray walls,
   Beside that shining hearth.
O peaceful scene of calm content!
Where happy faces came and went,
And heart with heart was closely blent,
   In sadness as in mirth!

I see them all: the aged sire
Deep in some book; the glowing fire
   Gleams on his silver hair.
The mother knits; her loving eye
Smiles on the children flitting by;
Her needles, clicking as they fly,
   Tell of her household care.

A group of stalwart boys I see,
Brimful of mirth—as boys will be—
   When evening tasks were done:
And—least of all—a little maid,
Her small head crowned with auburn braid,
Who, when the merry games were played,
   Was foremost in the fun.

How gay we were! What songs we sang,
Till the old walls with echoes rang,

While the wind roared without.
Again we sat, wide-eyed and pale,
And listened to some ancient tale—
How witches rode upon the gale,
  Or white ghosts roamed about.

'Twas long ago; those days are o'er:
I hear those songs no more, no more,
  Yet listen while I weep.
Time rules us all.   No joys abide.
That household band is scattered wide,
And some lie on the green hillside,
  Wrapped in a dreamless sleep.

FOUND—NOT TOO LATE.

FROM yonder church a wedding
  Came forth one day,
Only in this peculiar—
  It was late in the day;
For the locks of bride and bridegroom
  Were streaked with gray.

Their youth lay far behind them;
  Alone had tried
The up-grades of life's mountain
  This groom and bride.
They now clasped hands together
  On the down-hill side.

Broadly the stupid wondered;
  Yet, still and calm,
Sweet peace held close above them
  Her boughs of palm,
And touched the wounds of old battles
  With healing balm.

A year had passed.   At nightfall
  I saw them stand
At the door of a vine-wreathed cottage—

Hand held in hand—
While the tides of a crimson sunset
O'erflowed the land.

The crimson ebbed; the shadows
  Stole down the dell;
With its peaceful benediction,
  The twilight fell,
And the faint, sweet tone came floating
  Of a far-off bell.

I listened, and heard a sentence
  With meaning great.
The wife was whispering softly,
  " The perfect mate,
After long years of waiting,
  Found—not too late! "

A COUNTRY HOME.

A NOOK among the hills, a little farm,
  Whose fertile acres yield us daily bread:
A homely, low-browed dwelling, snug and
    warm,
  With wide blue country skies hung over-
    head.

No costly splendor here, no gilded glow;
  No dear-bought pictures hang upon the
    walls:
But bright and happy faces come and go,
  And through the windows God's sweet sun-
    shine falls.

We are not rich in heaps of hoarded gold:
  We are not poor, for we can keep at bay
The poor man's haunting spectres, want and
    cold,
  Can keep from owing debts we cannot pay.

With wholesome plenty is our table spread,
　With genial comfort glows our evening fire;
The fierce night-winds may battle over
　　head—
' Safe in our shelter, though the strife be dire.

When days grow long, and winter storms are
　　o'er,
　Here come the first birds of the early
　　spring,
And build their cunning nests beside the
　　door,
　Teaching sweet lessons as they work and
　　sing.

Here come our friends,—a dear and cherished
　　few,—
. Dearer, perchance, than if they numbered
　　more:
We greet them with a hand-clasp warm and
　　true,
　And give them of the best we have in store.

What though the rooms be small, and low
　　the roof?
　What though we can but offer simple fare?
It matters not; so Friendship's warp and
　　woof
　Are of spun gold, for these we need not
　　care.

We hear the great world surging like a sea,
　But the loud roar of winds and waves at
　　war,
Subdued by distance, comes melodiously,
　A soft and gentle murmur, faint and far.

We see the small go up, the great come down,
　And bless the peaceful safety of our lot,
The broken sceptre and the toppling crown,
　And crash of falling thrones—these shake
　us not.

We have some weary toil to struggle
  through,
Some trials, that we bravely strive to meet:
We have our sorrows, as all mortals do;
  We have our joys, too, pure, and calm,
  and sweet.

Is such a life too even in its flow?
  Too silent, calm, too barren of event?
Its very joys too still? I do not know;
  I think he conquers all, who wins content.

A DIRGE.

THE wind of Autumn blows,
  So cold, so cold;
The wind of Autumn blows,
Dead is the Summer rose,
  And the withered grass lies rotting on the
  mould.

The frost creeps round the door,
  So still, so still;
The frost creeps round the door,
The cricket sings no more,
  No more at twilight pleads the whip-po-
  will.

But I hear the owlet's cry,
  Forlorn, forlorn;
I hear the owlet's cry,
When the waning moon is high,
  And the raccoon's greedy call among the
  corn.

I mourn the Summer dead,
  So soon, so soon;
I mourn the Summer dead,
With all its glory fled,
  As I stand beneath the frosty waning moon.

And I think how life is going—
  So fast, so fast!
I think how life is going,
How swift its tides are flowing,
  How we scarcely hail our Summer, ere 'tis
  past.

THE WHIP-PO-WILL.

WHEN softly over field and town,
  And over yonder wood-crowned hill,
The twilight drops its curtain down,
  'Tis then we hear the whip-po-will.

From the near shadows sounds a call,
  Clear in its accent, loud and shrill;
And from the orchard's willow wall
  Comes the faint answer, "Whip-po-will."

The night creeps on; the summer-moon
  Whitens the roof and lights the sill;
And still the bird repeats his tune,
  His one refrain of "Whip-po-will."

We hear him not at morn or noon;
  Where hides he then so dumb and still?
Where lurks he, waiting for the moon?
  Who ever *saw* a whip-po-will?

Where plies his mate her household care?
  In what veiled nook, secure from ill,
Builds she the tiny cradle, where
  Nestles the baby whip-po-will?

I cannot tell,—yet prize the more
  The unseen bird, whose wild notes thrill
The evening-gloom about my door,—
  Still sweetly calling, "Whip-po-will."

Asleep through all the strong daylight,
  While other birds so gayly trill;
Waking to cheer the lonely night,—
  We love thee well, O whip-po-will!

THE THREAD OF GRAY.

I HAVE woven a braid, with patient toil—
   'Tis the work of many a day,
There are colors bright, but through them all
   Runs a thread of sober gray.

Blue and golden and green and red
   I have blended as best I may;
But through them all and binding them all
   Runs the thread of sober gray.

The blue and the gold twine out and in,
   Like rainbow tints astray;
Then brilliant strands of green and red—
   But always the thread of gray.

I know the colors will fade in the sun,
   Growing fainter day by day,
Till one from other you scarcely can tell;
   But fadeless the thread of gray.

And I think how like to an earnest life,
   With its pleasures by the way,
While through them all runs a steady aim,
   Like a thread of sober gray.

There are lights and laughter and feast and
     song,
   For labor must have its play—
But over and under and through them all
   Runs the thread of sober gray.

The mirth shall fail and the lights grow dim,
   And the song shall die away;
But the worker's crown shall be his who keeps
   To his thread of sober gray.

Alas for him who into his braid
   Weaves only the colors gay!
And alas for the close of the barren life
   That loses its thread of gray!

MY WILD-ROSE.

I HAD a garden, which I kept
   With busy hands and tender care;
And once, while carelessly I slept,
   Fanned softly by the drowsy air,
A wild-rose to my garden crept,
   And blossomed there.

O, sweet surprise! It seemed to me,
   Some fairy hand, my heart to bless,
Had brought it there, from wood or lea.
   It came unsought—'twas loved no less;
I stooped and touched it tenderly,
   With soft caress.

I grew to love it passing well:
   While strange exotics, rich and rare,
With heart of gold and crimson bell,
   Paid grudgingly for constant care,
My wild-rose, as in woodland dell,
   Bloomed fresh and fair.

I watered not, I did not prune,
   I tied it not with cord or thong;
Yet, morn by morn and noon by noon,
   Through days of summer, hot and long,
And underneath the midnight moon,
   From branches strong —

Hung clustered blossoms sweet and red;
   And day by day and week by week,
I trod the path which toward it led.
   Whate'er my mood, I did not speak,
But close against it bowed my head
   And pressed my cheek.

I think of it with sudden thrill!
   Now wide lands lie, deep water flows,
Smiles many a vale, looms many a hill
   Between me and the garden-close;
Yet fondly I remember still
   My sweet wild-rose.

TAR-AND-FEATHER REFORM.*

POUR the tar on, pour it thick;
Bring the feathers, make them stick
On her temples smooth and fair,
In the meshes of her hair:
There, now, shameless courtesan,
Charm your lovers if you can!

But the lovers—where are they?
Silently they slink away.
Boys must sow wild-oats, you know;
Scold them well and let them go,
Boys are boys; to err is human—
Tar-and-feathers for the woman!

Woman? she is but a child.
Well, no matter; drive her wild.
Young and fair? so much the worse!
Brand her deeper, let the curse
On her young head weighing down,
Crush her, force her on the town.

She is fallen, that's enough,
Give her, henceforth, kick and cuff.
While we work and pray and weep
For the heathen o'er the deep,
We are saints of purity—
We are Christians—don't you see?

When we women have our way,
When it comes—that glorious day—
When we sit in honor great,
Piloting the ship of State,
All shall then, as well as we,
Practice this our theory:

Never right a sinking boat,
When a woman is afloat;

* Written after the women of a town in Iowa had mobbed
and tarred-and-feathered a young girl of sixteen.

If her record holds a flaw,
Do not throw her e'en a straw;
Kick her roughly, push her down;
Hold her under, let her drown!

AN EVENING MONOLOGUE.

FRIEND of my soul, come, sit by me
  In this evening calm, with the sun gone
  down.   `
While the wide west glows like a crimson
  sea,
  Flooding with splendor the fields and the
  town.

Talk if you will, or idly dream,
  With your gaze on the track of the van-
  ished sun.
Our thoughts shall blend though silent the
  stream;
  Speech and silence to us are one.

Up from the south comes a breath of spring;
  It flutters your beard and it lifts your hair;
Yonder a robin, with folded wing,
  Sits and sings in the branches bare.

Sweet hour of peace! on the prairies brown,
  On the quiet homestead's dun-gray walls,
On the silent lanes, on the distant town,
  Like a benediction the twilight falls.

Slowly, softly, the roseate glow
  Pales, yet lingers; the robin's tune
Is hushed to silence; a silver bow
  Hangs on high—'tis the white new moon.

The moments pass. See that moving gleam!
  Nearer it comes, swift, weirdly bright;
And a train, life-laden, with eerie scream,
  Sweeps down the valley into the night.

The moments pass.   We are wrapped about
  With thickening shadows; one by one,
In the deep, dark blue, the stars shine out.
  Night and silence—the day is done.

Oft have we watched the daylight fade,
  But a time must come we know—the last.
And the sweep of the years will not bo
    stayed;
  That on-coming night is hastening fast.

Once, then, to watch while the darkness
    creeps,
  And you or I—oh! which shall it be?—
Must wake and weep while the other sleeps,
  Old and alone—ah, me! ah, me!

DAYS WE REMEMBER.

Days that glide in an even rhyme
To which our feet keep steady time—
    Be they in May or December;—
Days when life is a summer sea,
Whereon our ships rock dreamily;
Days when an easy round of care,
Is all the load that our shoulders bear;
Days that a calm succession keep
Of peaceful labor and peaceful sleep;
Days that serenely slip away,
With little of sorrow, yet scarcely gay;—
    Are not the days wo remember.

Days that are fraught with throbs of bliss,
With love's caress, with love's close kiss—
    Be they in May or December;—
Days when rush through our wilderness
Whelming torrents of happiness;
Days when the heart, in its joyous swell,
Beats and throbs like a festive bell;
And days, oh! days when we sit alone
With dumb, white lips that make no moan,

By close-sealed vaults, whose chambers cold
Our loveliest, dearest treasures hold;
When, as the heavy hours drag by,
We long—and long in vain—to die;—
    These are the days we remember.

THE SLEEPING VILLAGE.

THE village sleeps; the moonbeams fall,
Pale, still, and cold, on roof and wall,
    And flood the empty street.
How still! The dust lies all unstirred;
No sound of rolling wheels is heard,
    No tread of passing feet.

Where traffic hurried to and fro,
Only the night-winds come and go,
    Whirling the dead leaves by.
The cold lake laps its pebbled shore;
And round each closely-bolted door
    The frost creeps silently.

The village sleeps—O blessed rest!
With hard hands folded on its breast,
    Lies overburdened Toil;
Grief smiles in dreams, its woe forgot;
Pale Want forgets its dreary lot;
    The springs of Care uncoil.

The fevers that infest the day
Yield to the night, and sink away
    To pulses soft and even.
E'en Joy is still; Love nestles deep
In clasping arms, whose touch makes sleep
    A calm as sweet as Heaven.

The night grows deeper; colder falls
The moonlight on the silent walls;
    Still creeps the stealthy frost;
And deeper grows the calm of rest
In throbbing brain and troubled breast,
    By day so passion-tost.

O blessings priceless, Night and Sleep!
Did never close the eyes that weep;
  Did struggle never cease;
Did ne'er the balm of Rest come down
Upon the weary, toiling town—
  Then death were sole release.

A BRIDE OF A DAY.

OH! sing a song, in low soft notes—
 Tender, and sweet, and sad—
For her who lies all pallid, still,
 In her last garments clad.

A fair young bride of but a day—
 (Sing low, sing soft and low)—
And yet, and yet her bed must be
 Under the drifting snow.

Under the drifting snow—ah me—
 To lie in her frozen sleep,
While love, bereft, with empty arms,
 Is left to wake and weep.

But yestermorn, how bright her smile!
 How soft the blush that rose,
Mantling the white of neck and brow,
 As sunset tints the snows.

With tender light her dark eyes shone;
 Sweet was the roseate glow;
Alas! how little thought we then,
 Her sun had dipped so low.

Through all the hours one mourner sits,
 Watching her pulseless rest,
With dumb, white lips and hopeless look,
 And head bowed on his breast.

Ah, death! thy ways are dark and strange—
 Passing age, sorrow by,
While youth and joy along thy track
 All scathed and blasted lie.

FARMER JOHN.

" If I'd nothing to do," said Farmer John,
   " To fret or to bother me—
Were I but rid of this mountain of work, .
   What a good man I could be!

" The pigs get out, and the cows get in,
   Where they have no right to be;
And the weeds in the garden and in the
    corn—
   Why, they fairly frighten me.

" It worries me out of temper quite,
   And well-nigh out of my head.
What a curse it is that a man must toil
   Like this for his daily bread!"

But Farmer John he broke his leg,
   And was kept for many a week
A helpless and an idle man;—
   Was he therefore mild and meek?

Nay; what with the pain, and what with the
    fret
   Of sitting with nothing to do—
And the farmwork botched by a shiftless
    hand,
   He got very cross and blue.

He scolded the children and cuffed the dog
   That fawned about his knee;
And snarled at his wife, though she was kind
   And patient as wife could be.

He grumbled and whined and fretted and
    fumed,
   The whole of the long day through.
" 'Twill ruin me quite," cried Farmer John,
   " To sit here with nothing to do!"

But time wore on, and he thoughtful grew,
  As he watched his patient wife,
And he vowed one morn with a tear in his
    eye,
  He would lead a different life.

His hurt got well, and he went to work;
  And a busier man than he,
A happier man, or a pleasanter man,
  You never would wish to see.

The pigs got out, and he drove them back,
  Whistling right merrily;
He mended the fence, and kept the cows
  Just where they ought to be.

Weeding the garden was jolly fun,
  And ditto hoeing the corn.
" I'm happier far," said Farmer John,
  " Than I've been since I was born."

He learned a lesson that lasts him well;—
  'Twill last him his whole life through.
He frets but seldom, and never because
  He has plenty of work to do.

"I tell you what," says Farmer John,
  " They are either knaves or fools
Who long to be idle, for idle hands
  Are the Devil's chosen tools! "

BEAUTIFUL THINGS.

BEAUTIFUL faces are those that wear—
It matters little if dark or fair—
Whole-souled honesty printed there.

Beautiful eyes are those that show,
Like crystal panes where hearth-fires glow,
Beautiful thoughts that burn below.

Beautiful lips are those whose words
Leap from the heart like songs of birds,
Yet whose utterance prudence girds.

Beautiful hands are those that do
Work that is earnest and brave and true,
Moment by moment the long day through.

Beautiful feet are those that go
On kindly ministries to and fro—
Down lowliest ways, if God wills it so.

Beautiful shoulders are those that bear
Ceaseless burdens of homely care
With patient grace and with daily prayer.

Beautiful lives are those that bless—
Silent rivers and happiness,
Whose hidden fountains but few may guess.

Beautiful twilight, at set of sun,
Beautiful goal with race well won,
Beautiful rest, with work well done.

Beautiful graves, where grasses creep,
Where brown leaves fall, where drifts lie deep
Over worn-out hands—oh beautiful sleep!

THE WILD-ROSE.

Peeping from out the hedges,
    Bending above the brim
Of the stream that threads the meadows,
    Fringing the forest dim.

Stealing into my garden,
    Waiting not for my call;
Scaling the ancient gateway,
    Creeping under the wall.

Climbing the mossed enclosure
    Yonder, where willows wave,
Nestling against the tombstone,
    Clustered on every grave.

Cherished by none, yet blooming
    Silently everywhere;
Asking for naught, yet giving,
    Lavish as summer air.

I *love* thee, rose of the hedges,
   Rose of the streamlet's rim;
Meek adorner of tombstones,
   Fringe of the forest dim.

KNITTING.

An old-time kitchen, an open door,
Sunshine lying across the floor;
A little maid, feet bare and brown,
Cheeks like roses, a cotton gown,
Rippling masses of shining hair,
And a childish forehead smooth and fair.

The child is knitting. The open door
Wooes her, tempts her, more and more.
The sky is cloudless, the air is sweet,
And sadly restless the bare brown feet.
Still, as she wishes her task were done,
She counts the rounds off, one by one.

Higher yet mounts the sun of June;
But one round more!—A joyous tune
Ripples out from the childish lips,
While swift and swifter the finger-tips
Play out and in, till I hear her say,
"Twenty rounds! I'm going to play!"

Up to the hedge where the sweet-brier blows,
Down to the bank where the brooklet flows,
Chasing the butterflies, watching the bees,
Wading in clover up to her knees,
Mocking the bobolinks; oh, what fun
It is to be free when the task is done!

Years and years have glided away,
The child is a woman, and threads of gray
One by one creep into her hair,
And I see the prints of the feet of care.
Yet I like to watch her. To-night she sits
By her household fire, and as then she knits.

Swiftly the needles glance, and the thread
Glides through her fingers, white and red.
'Tis a baby's stocking. To and fro,
And out and in as the needles go,
She sings as she sang that day in June,
But the low, soft strain is a nursery tune.

Close beside her the baby lies,
Slowly closing his sleepy eyes.
Forward, backward, the cradle swings,
Touched by her foot as she softly sings.
And now in silence her watch she keeps;
The song is hushed, for the baby sleeps.

Up from the green, through the twilight gray,
Come the shouts of a troop at play.
Blue eyes, black eyes, golden curls—
These are all hers—her boys and girls.
Then wonder not at the prints of care,
Or the silver threads in her braided hair.

Does she ever pine for the meadow brook,
The sweet-brier hedge, the clover nook?
When sweet winds woo, when smiles the sun,
Does she ever wish that her task was done?
Would you know? Then watch her where
    she sits,
Smiling dreamily, while she knits.

SEPTEMBER.

'Tis Autumn in our Northern land.
    The Summer walks a Queen no more;
Her sceptre drops from out her hand;
    Her strength is spent, her passion o'er.
On lake and stream, on field and town,
The placid sun smiles calmly down.

The teeming Earth its fruit has borne;
    The grain-fields lie all shorn and bare;
And where the serried ranks of corn
    Waved proudly in the summer-air,

And bravely tossed their yellow locks,
Now thickly stand the bristling shocks.

On sunny slope, on crannied wall
  The grapes hang purpling in the sun;
Down to the turf the brown nuts fall,
  And golden, apples one by one.
Our bins run o'er with ample store—
Thus Autumn reaps what Summer bore.

The mill turns by the waterfall;
  The loaded wagons go and come;
All day I hear the teamster's call,
  All day I hear the thresher's hum;
And many a shout and many a laugh
Come breaking through the clouds of chaff.

Gay, careless sounds of homely toil!
  With mirth and labor closely blent,
The weary tiller of the soil
  Wins seldom wealth, but oft content.
'Tis better still if he but knows
What sweet, wild beauty round him glows.

The brook glides toward the sleeping lake—
  Now babbling over shining stones;
Now under clumps of bush and brake,
  Hushing its brawl to murmuring tones;
And now it takes its winding path
Through meadows green with aftermath.

The frosty twilight early falls,
  But household fires burn warm and red.
The cold may creep without the walls,
  And growing things lie stark and dead—
No matter, so the hearth be bright
When household faces meet at night.

A DREAM.

I DREAMED a dream in a winter night,
  When sullen winds blew about the door,
And over the snow-fields, cold and white,
  And through the forests with muffled roar.

Through all the wintry sounds, I heard
   The rustle of a tiny wing;
And wildly carolled a dear brown bird—
   The bird that sings at the gates of Spring.

My pulses leaped in a sudden thrill!
   Was the Winter gone? I thought in my
     sleep—
Had the Spring come in with that silvery trill?
   Would storms no longer their wassails
     keep?

I woke—and there came, in frosty bars,
   The light of a pale and filmy moon,
And the far, faint twinkle of misty stars;
   And cold winds chanted their midnight
     tune.

Gone was the rustle of tiny wing;
   Silent the song of the dear brown bird;
Closely barred stood the gates of Spring,
   And the chant of the winds was all I heard!

So the pilgrim dreams; and he hears afar
   The harps of gold; and the radiant gleam
Comes flashing through the gates ajar
   Of the Sea of Glass, and the Crystal Stream.

But he wakes; and closed are the pearly
     gates;
   Gone is the music, the flash and gleam;
But he goes his way, and in patience waits—
   He goes his way, but he keeps his dream!

A SONG OF PEACE.

SING me a song to-night,
   Not sad, nor yet keyed to mirth;
But a household lay, in a soothing voice,
   As the cricket sings on the hearth.

No loud high-soaring strains,
 When body and brain are spent;
But I long to listen with half-shut lids,
 To a song of sweet content.

Let the notes drop from your lips,
 Like summer rain from the eaves,
Or the dreamy tinkle of far-off bells
 That comes through whispering leaves.

Let me hold your hand the while—
 Your hand so firm and fine;
Its soft, warm clasp is a touch of peace,
 And its pulses shall quiet mine.

Sing on, so soft and low;
 Dispelled by the soothing strain,
Gone the heat from my throbbing brow,
 And the ache from heart and brain.

Sing on; your breath at my cheek,
 Your hand still clasping mine;
Your voice and your touch, my household
 bird,
 Are sweeter and better than mine.

DON'T YOU TELL.

If you have a cherished secret,
 Don't you tell:—
Not your friend—for his tympanum
 Is a bell,
With its echoes, wide-rebounding,
Multiplied and far-resounding,—
 Don't you tell.

If, yourself, you cannot keep it,
 Then, who can?
Could you more expect of any
 Other man?
Yet you put him, if he tells it,
If he gives away or sells it,
 Under ban.

Sell your gems to any buyer
    In the mart:
Of your wealth, to feed the hungry,
    Spare a part.
Blessings on the open pocket!
But your secret—keep it, lock it
    In your heart.

ACCEPTANCE.

THAT man is wisest who accepts his lot,
    Yet mends it where he can—glad if there
    grows
Some lowly flower beside his lonely cot,
    E'en while he plants and tends his Alpine
    rose.

Some good comes to us all.   No poverty
    But has some precious gift laid at its door.
We scorn it, call it small; what fools are we,
    To spurn the less because it is not more!

There are some thirsty souls, all sick and
    faint
    With longing for the cup that is denied.
Would they but stoop and drink, without
    complaint,
    From the near stream, and so be satisfied.

There are some hungry hearts that well nigh
    break
    With the dull soreness of mere emptiness.
To fill the void and soothe the weary ache,
    Let them but strive some other hearts to
    bless.

There are some idle hands that reach afar
    For wider mission, some great work of
    fame.
Would they but grapple in life's daily war,
    Reward awaits them, nobler than a name.

O thirsty souls! O hungry hearts, and
    hands,
Weary with idleness! take what you may
Of proffered good; accept life as it stands,
    And make the most of its swift-fleeting
    day.

DEEP WATERS.

LAUGHING and shouting its rocks among,
    The brook threads the upland lea:
But, for all its song so loudly sung,
And the small uproar of its babbling tongue,
    'Tis a shallow thing in its glee.

Solemn and still doth the river go,
    As it winds through its vale of rest:
Calm in its mien and its tide is slow;
Smooth is its face and its voice is low—
    Yet fleets may ride on its breast.

Oh! the river is great in its silent might,
    As it rolleth eternally:
But, with all its calm, so still, so bright,
In a passionate longing, day and night,
    It stretcheth its hands to the sea.

The brook and the river are each a life;
    And the one all men may know;
For its fretful current with noise is rife,
And its grief and joy, and its petty strife,
    Are seen in its shallow flow.

The other so peaceful seems, so still;
    And we fancy a soul at rest:
But, little we know what strength of will,
What mighty pulses, that throb and thrill,
    Are hid in a silent breast.

A clear, cool eye, with a changeless glow,
    The clasp of a steady palm,
May cover a tide that sweeps below,
In a strong, a resistless undertow,
    Yet we say, "How cool and calm!"

SHADOWS.

Gray, cold and gray
  Is the desolate winter sky.
As the colorless daylight fades away
  And a starless night draws nigh,
I sit in my darkening room
  By the fire,—it is burning low,
While Fancy weaves in her pauseless loom,
And swift and silent, amid the gloom,
  Her shuttle glides to and fro.

Sad, sombre and sad
  Is the web that she weaves to-night;
And it wraps my soul as the world is clad
  In the desolate evening light.
Strange is this nameless sorrow!
  I weep, and I scarce know why.
Is it the frown of some dark to-morrow
That looms above me, and must I borrow
  Grief from the by-and-by?

Why, Fancy, why
  Hast thou done so ill thy task?
Instead of a gloom like the starless sky,
  Oh, give me the thing I ask.
It is just as easy to rear
  A sunny castle in Spain
As to conjure up some shape of fear,
Some shadowy grief that wrings a tear
  From the ache of a nameless pain.

TO MRS. C. H. PHILLIPS.

Brave woman, treading, with unfaltering
    feet,
  A path of sorrow, wet with many a tear,
Sustaining, with a courage rare and sweet,
  Your heavy weight of grief, so hard to
    bear;

A sister greets you. Could my lips but speak
  In language sweet and tender, strong and
    true,
All the full sympathies that utterance seek,
  Some crumb of comfort it might bring to
    you.

I know you well. I mark your sunny face,
  Your bright and kindly smile, your cheer-
    ful tone;
Yet, hidden close within its sacred place,
  I know that patient grief still holds its
    throne.

All that your friends can give you gladly
  · take;
  You bid them welcome to your lovely
    home;
And yet your heart still holds its weary ache,
  Its darkened chambers where no friend can
    come.

The lonely night, with dreams of pleasures
    past,
  The waking but to feel they are no more;
The long, long days (they once did fly so
    fast!)
  The sense of dreary loss, the longing sore;

I know all these; and yet I know that Time—
  Time, the dread spoiler—hath a touch of
    healing.
O'er cherished graves snow falls, and winter
    rime;
  Cool grasses creep, and moss comes softly
    stealing.

Earth hath a tender clasp. In slumber deep
  Folds she our dear ones to her peaceful
    breast.
For them all trial ends; so, let us weep
  Few bitter tears o'er their untroubled rest.

No need that we forget; let grief pass by,
　While we live o'er the tender, precious
　　hours,
The touch, the kiss—so dear to memory.
　These are our own—sweet, never-fading
　　flowers.

Sad are our partings, dark the night of sor-
　row;
　Yet blest are we, if hope descry the dawn;
If faith reach forward to a sweet to-morrow,
　Whose joys await us when the night is
　　gone.

FRIENDS THAT I USED TO KNOW.

THE storm of the day is past;
　The rain has a fainter sound;
Yet low-hung clouds their misty skirts
　Trail over the sodden ground.

The heavy twilight falls;
　The clouds trail more and more,
And the early darkness stealthily creeps
　Up to the farmhouse door.

I sit, in the gathering night,
　By the fire—it is burning low—
And think, with a longing akin to pain,
　Of the friends that I used to know.

And a thrilling vision sweeps
　Through the chambers of my brain;
Gone are the mist, the darkening room,
　And the prairies, soaked with rain.

I see the friends I love,
　(I shall love them evermore)
And I look in their eyes and clasp their
　hands,
　Beneath a vine-wreathed door.

Yonder are wood-crowned hills,
   Flaming with gold and red:
I hear the brawl of a fretting brook,
   Swollen high in its rocky bed.

The orchard, the willow hedge,
   The pasture with cows, and the well,
The giant hickory near the gate,
   On guard, like a sentinel.

I see all these, as I stand
   In the autumn sunset's glow,
And talk and listen, with throbbing heart,
   To the friends I used to know.

I start—and the vision fades,
   The fire is dead,. and the light
Is gone from the dripping and darkened
    panes:
   I sit alone in the night.

DICK AND I.

I HAD a lover once—'twas long ago—
I must have been some eight or nine, or so,
And he perhaps was ten. He had blue eyes,
And hair like cotton-weed, that floats and
    flies,
Or—better, like a hank of bleachen flax.
He was not handsome—but, I'm telling
    "fax,"
And must be accurate. A "poet's lie"
May always be æsthetic—reason why—
The poet paints from out his own invention,
While I—I've only actual truths to mention.

I loved him. If all else were homely prose,
There's poetry in that. A bright red rose
Creeps through a cranny in a naked wall,
And blossoms there;—it is a rose, for all.

My rose bloomed early, and its growth was
    quick—
Much like a mushroom's. Ah, white-headed
    Dick!
If this should meet your eye, you will re-
    member
One rainy day—'twas in the gray November.

A monstrous kettle hanging from the crane,
With steam clouds rolling up to meet the
    rain;
A great old fireplace, with wide open maw;
Two children sucking cider through a straw;
Such was the tableau; as the night closed in,
The firelight with the darkness fought to win,
Pushing the shadows back against the walls,
Where bacon hung, dried apples, coats and
    shawls.

The night grew darker. Still the autumn
    rain
Beat with its wet hands on the window pane;
But we two liked it well. We put together
Our two small heads, and sagely on the
    weather
Exchanged congratulations. No moonlight.
The steady rain—sure, Dick must stay all
    night.

We had it settled, and we went to play.
"Blindfold," "I spy," and even "Pull
    away,"
Came on in turn. The evening was near
    spent,
And nought had troubled our complete con-
    tent;
But perfect happiness—we grasp it, fold it,
Thinking it ours, alas! we never hold it
For any length of time. It slips, and quivers,
And something hits and knocks it into shiv-
    ers.

And this is what hit ours—this the shock
That fell upon our peace at nine o'clock.
Fate lifted up its hand so hard and grim,
And struck this blow: *Dick's mother sent for
   him!*

He cried, and so did I. Ah well,
It is a simple story that I tell,
And you may laugh, perchance—yet it is
   real,
And serves to show the griefs that children
   feel,
Which grown folks do not count on. I have
   seen
Since then some sorrow, some pangs sharp
   and keen;
Have even dreamed I stood at Heaven's door,
And saw it shut on me forevermore.
Yet that one night, so gloomy, and so wet,
With rain and tears, I've not forgotten yet.

SEEING THE EDITORS.

I WENT to see the Editors, in great Milwaukee
   town,
And some were old, with hoary hair, some
   young, with locks of brown,
But, old or young, or tall or short, when all
   was said and done,
They seemed a goodly set of men as e'er the
   sun shone on.

They had come from north and south, they
   had come from east and west,
Down from the northern pine lands, up from
   the prairie's breast.
Men of the Leading Journals, men of the
   Local Sheet,
Came flocking in together, and I watched
   them meet and greet.

At this I greatly wondered; I saw each meet
    the other,
With a smile and a clasping hand, as if he
    were his brother.
Fair words and kindly cheer were the order
    of the day;
The pipe of peace went round, and the sword
    was laid away.

"Are these men friends or enemies?" I
    questioned silently;
I recalled the odious names they have called
    each other by,—
"Idiot," "knave," and "sorehead"—all
    these, and many more,
They have used to pelt each other—is their
    rancor spent and o'er?

They talked of their position, of the duty of
    the press;
How opponents should be treated—with hon-
    est friendliness.
A fair and lovely theory! the practice seems
    to be
To call each man a rascal, who don't agree
    with me.

What do they mean, I wonder, by the "free-
    dom of the press?"
Is it this,—that each is free to vent his "cuss-
    edness?"   [to be
Free to ban and blacken whoever may chance
On the other side of the fence?—O glorious
    liberty!

But here they were—these warriors who have
    oft each other flayed,—
Talking in tones fraternal as they drank their
    lemonade;
And I wondered if the time, so long foretold,
    had come,—
The day of peace and brotherhood—the great
    Millennium.

I have read the papers since, and I see my
    hope was vain;
For the hatchet that was buried, they have
    dug it up again;
The sword has left its scabbard, the spiked
    guns roar away,
And he who was a " sorehead," is a " sore-
    head " to-day.

Each man is at his desk; he has grasped the
    wires again,
And is pulling for his party, with all his
    might and main.
Opponents thrash each other, who shook
    hands the other day;
And I question,—do they mean *one-half* of
    what they say?

THE FIRST BIRD.

THE south wind blows with a hint of spring—
    A prophecy—it can be nothing more;
But there sits a bird with wee brown wing,
    Up in the hickory, over the door.

On a naked twig he sits and sings;
    And the March sun shines, and the warm
    winds blow,
And his frail perch trembles and sways and
    swings,
    Over great masses of melting snow.

Oh! his song is sweet! and almost I think
    That the spring is come; and a conjured
    scene
Of the planting of corn and the bobolink,
    Dreamily rises my thoughts between.

But heavy and deep lies the winter drift!—
    Ah, little bird, you're ahead of your time!
The wind will change with a sudden shift;
    You will shiver and chill in our northern
    clime.

6

You had better have stayed in the orange
    trees
For some days yet—for where will you go
When the icy rain-drops fall and freeze?
    And where will you hide from the sleet and
    snow?

Little bird, would you only come to my door,
    I would take you into my kitchen warm—
Where strangers a welcome have found be-
    fore—
    And keep you safe from the driving storm.

Will you come?—But you still believe in the
    spring;
    You slight the offer I make, and me.
You are off! with your song and your glanc-
    ing wing,
    And silent and bare is my hickory tree.

OUR FRIENDSHIP.

THEY say true friendship changeth not,
    But grows and grows;
Through chance, and time, and treacherous
    plot,
Through change of scene and change of lot,
    Still changeless shows.

If this be true, sure here is seen
    Some great mistake!
The friend of years no friend hath been,
Else naught on earth could come between,
    The bond to break.

Am I, then, false? I meant no lie;
    Yet nevermore
With friendship on my lip, can I,
As oft aforetime, seek thine eye,
    Or cross thy door!

Dost marvel why? 'Tis quickly told.
  Here at thy feet
I fling away our friendship old,
Because henceforth our two hearts hold
  A tie more sweet!

I love thee! therefore can we be
  No longer friends.
Thou takest what I offer thee—
Thy whole heart's sweetness givest me.
  So friendship ends.

DREAMS.

WHEN the sun is shining o'er us,
   And our duties lie before us,
We lay our wishes by on secret shelves;
    In their napkins, wrapped securely,
    We enfold them, thinking surely
They are hidden both from others and our-
  selves.

   But when Slumber sweetly holds us,
    And in velvet arms enfolds us,
And the moonlight through the curtain faintly
  streams;
    Then from out their hiding-places,
    Clad in soft, bewitching graces,
Come our wishes to inspire and rule our
  dreams.

   How they haunt the midnight pillow!
    How the pulse swells, like a billow,
As the dreamer clasps the thing he most de-
  sires!
    And his throbbing heart rejoices
    As he hears enchanting voices
Singing, keeping rhythmic time to golden
  lyres.

Wants he riches? power? honor?
Fancy is a lavish donor,
All he craves bestowing on his longing soul.
　　Oh, the ripe, delicious sweetness!
　　Oh, the rare and rich completeness,
As he quaffs with thirsty lips the brimming
　　bowl!

　　But alas! the sudden waking,
　　When above the hill tops breaking,
With its weary burdens bringing, comes the
　　day!
　　Then the dreamer grasps the real,
　　Puts aside his sweet ideal,
Deftly hides his dream within its nook away.

A MORNING CALL.

Come in and welcome, tiny thing,
With snowy breast and soft brown wing,
　　And beak of tawny hue.
But why, I pray, this wild alarm?
I will not let you come to harm;
　　I'm fond of such as you.

Stop, little bird! you foolish thing!
Why will you beat your tender wing
　　Against the cruel pane?
I do the same myself; I fret
Against the bounds about me set,
　　And find it all in vain.

I cannot make you understand.
Wait—I will take you in my hand,
　　And put you through the door.
You precious, panting little mite!
The cat would eat you at a bite,
　　And lick his jaws for more.

He shall not have you, nor will I
Keep you from yonder clear blue sky.

There! soar where'er you list.
To cage a bird breaks Nature's laws;
And then I am and always was
　　An abolitionist.

Go, find your mate; she waits for you
Somewhere in yonder fields of blue,
　　Or on some swaying bough.
Tell her you got into a scrape,
But made a fortunate escape—
　　And please just tell her how.

You might have met a prisoner's doom,
When you came blundering to my room;
　　Yet I have set you free.
Then, sometimes fold your wee brown wing
Upon my hickory tree, and sing
　　Your sweetest song to me.

DAY BY DAY.

THOU askest what may my mission be,
And what great work I am bound to do;
Alas! I cannot unfold to thee
The work of a day till that day be through.

I know not at night what awaits at morn;
I know not at morn what the noon shall bring;
Nor know, till the eve its fruit has borne,
What the twilight folds in its dusky wing.

I purpose and plan, but cannot dispose;
The work I would do slips through my hands;
I am given a task that I never chose:
And my strength is fettered by bars and
　　bands.

I purpose and plan, yet blindly go,
Doubtful whither; to reach my end
I sturdily toil, yet well I know
To the will of events my will must bend.

I would build me a tower, with lordly walls,
On a lofty rock that o'ertops the lands;
But, ere it is finished, my structure falls,
For the rock has crumbled to shifting sands.

I have woven a web with the toil of years;
I have laid it by, forgetting the moth:
And I thread my needle and sharpen my
    shears;
But lo! the worms have eaten the cloth.

Shall I then do naught; shall I sit in sloth,
Because has tumbled my lordly tower?
And because the worms have eaten my cloth—
Scorning the calls of the present hour?

If, day by day, while keen desire
Pants for the work that is great and grand,
Some small, sweet task by the household-fire
Mutely appeals to my brain and hand,

Shall I then complain? Shall I turn away,
Closing my heart to the tender call?
And leave undone the work of to-day,
Because it is humble, unseen, and small?

Nay; for, better than sounding name,
And better than riches, that rot and rust,
And better than glistening wreaths of fame,
That wither, and crumble, and fall to dust,

Are the blessings that come to me, one by
    one,
The peaceful joys that enter my gate,
If I do my duty from sun to sun,
Be it lowly or high, be it small or great.

The sweet, glad smile in a loved one's eye,
The tender cadence of household-tones,
Are better than crowns of the great and
    high;—
For to live on pride is to feed on stones.

TWO FAREWELLS.

I HAVE bidden two of my neighbors
   A long farewell to-day.
Both were going a journey,
   And both were going to stay.

One, with eyes that were misty,
   Like skies all heavy with rain,
Said, "In the years that are coming,
   We may somewhere meet again."

She was bound for Dakotah;
   And, watching the wagons go—
White-covered, heavily laden,
   Clogged with the early snow.

I thought of the bleak, cold prairies,
   Of the toil, for many a day,
With the storms of wild November
   Howling along the way.

The other lay cold and silent;
   Said naught, nor clasped my hand;
And yet we were friends—ah, speechless
   Men go to the Silent Land!

Mute, and pale, and speechless,
   This wild October day,
He passed down into the shadows—
   Into the shadows gray.

And he has finished his journey;
   The pain and the toil are o'er;
Nobly he wrought his life-work,
   Bravely his burdens bore.

To-night the winds are raving;
   The snow falls over his head;
Yet he turns not on his pillow,
   Stirs not in his lowly bed.

So gone are two of my neighbors;
　Empty their places stand.
One is gone to Dakotah,
　And one to the Silent Land.

HARVEST-HOME.

AGAIN the Harvest-Home.　Night after night,
　The full, round moon climbs up the dusky
　　East,
Ere yet the day quite yields its throne to night,
　Ere yet the sunset-glow has wholly ceased.

Night follows night in glorious, stately march.
　The same round moon, the same far, dusky
　　stars,
In solemn splendor, from the vaulted arch
　Shed their soft light in pale and misty bars.

Do　you　remember　one　sweet　Summer's
　　prime—
　Such nights as these, such dim and dusky
　　glow—
When　first　our　two　lives　met　in　blended
　　rhyme ?
　We both were young—and it was long ago.

What hope was ours, as, standing hand in
　　hand,
　Amid the Summer-moon's soft, tender light,
We　wove　our　plans　together,　strand　by
　　strand,
　In fearless faith?　How is it, Love, to-night?

As then, the whispering winds steal　through
　　the corn:
　As then, we hear the owl's weird solemn cry;
As then, the tawny fields, but newly shorn,
　Wet with the night-dews, bare and silent lie.

As then, the bark of dogs sounds faint and
    far;
    As then, the thick grass hides an insect
      throng;
As then, the glowworm shows its tiny star;
    As then, rings sharp and clear the cricket's
     song.

As then, the solemn moonlight, shining down,
    Blent with the twilight's last departing ray.
Then seems but now—and yet your locks
    were brown,
    And now I see them thickly strewn with
    gray.

Then seems but now. I feel the same dear
    arm
    That then I leaned upon, about me thrown;
The voice that swayed me with its subtle
    charm
    Still keeps for me the old caressing tone.

Then seems but now—and yet your steps are
    slow;
    Your brow shows prints of pain, and toil,
    and care;
And I have seen my youth's last roses blow.
    I, too, am growing old—why should I care ?

What matters it ? In counting off our life
    By harvest-moons, the checkered, toilsome
    years
Show in their record more of peace than strife,
    More joy than sorrow, more of smiles than
    tears.

Time flies apace. Spring-flowers, and Winter-
    rime,
    And sweet June roses, swiftly go and come;
Yet the full richness of our youthful prime
    Still crowns us both anew at Harvest-Home.

THE PITY OF IT.

IT seems so strange to watch the crowd
　　That gathers on some festal day,
To mark the lowly and the proud,
　　Aglow with mirth, and think that they
　　Are but a throng of masquers gay.

'Tis true that some show signs of grief;
　　Yon sad-eyed widow wears her weeds;
Yon mother mourns her fallen leaf,
　　And tells you how her bosom bleeds.

Yon soldier, battered in the wars,
　　Moving with painful step, and slow,
Limps proudly, proudly wears his scars;—
　　Such hurts as these all men may know.

But deeper sorrow, keener throes,
　　Are hidden by a careless smile,
And laughter on the lip, the while
　　The heart is torn and no one knows.

The pity of this earthly life
　　Is, that the deepest heartaches lie
　　Beyond the reach of sympathy;
The sorest wounds are got in strife
　　Waged in the dark, where none may see,
Oft hiding still the rankling knife
　　That tortures with slow misery.

I see my neighbor come and go
　　With airy speech and smiling lip;
I call him gay—I little know
　　What unseen hand, with deadly grip
Clutches his heart, what torture slow
Wears out his life, while borne alone,
　As ceaseless dropping wears a stone.

If floods destroy, if fires consume,
　　Full hands reach out in charity;
Across misfortune's darkest gloom
　　Shine kindly rays of sympathy;

If a friend dies a tolling bell
May to the world the story tell.
　　But deeper griefs than these there be—
　　The death's head in the closet hid
Is ghastlier than the still white face,
Or the cold hands, in waxen grace
　　Lying beneath the coffin lid.

A living woe from mortal eyes
　　Is curtained close; the direst strife
Is in the breast—And herein lies
　　The pity of this earthly life.

LITTLE THINGS.

WE call him strong who stands unmoved—
　　Calm as some tempest-beaten rock—
　　When some great trouble hurls its shock;
We say of him, His strength is proved:
　　But, when the spent storm folds its wings,
　　How bears he then Life's little things?

About his brow we twine our wreath
　　Who seeks the battle's thickest smoke,
　　Braves flashing gun and sabre-stroke,
And scoffs at danger, laughs at death;
　　We praise him till the whole land rings;
　　But—is he brave in little things?

We call him great who does some deed
　　That echo bears from shore to shore,—
　　Does that, and then does nothing more:
Yet would his work earn richer meed,
　　When brought before the King of kings,
　　Were he but great in little things.

We closely guard our castle-gates
　　When great temptations loudly knock,
　　Draw every bolt, clinch every lock,
And sternly fold our bars and gates:
　　Yet some small door wide open swings
　　At the sly touch of little things.

I can forgive—'tis worth my while—
　　The treacherous blow, the cruel thrust;
　　Can bless my foe, as Christian must,
While Patience smiles her royal smile:
　　Yet quick resentment fiercely slings
　　Its shots of ire at little things.

And I can tread beneath my feet
　　The hills of Passion's heaving sea,
　　When wind-tossed waves roll stormily:
Yet scarce resist the siren sweet
　　That at my heart's door softly sings
　　"Forget, forget Life's little things."

But what *is* Life?　Drops make the sea;
　　And petty cares and small events,
　　Small causes and small consequents,
Make up the sum for you and me:
　　Then, O for strength to meet the stings
　　That arm the points of little things!

BECALMED.

　　Adrift in my little boat,
　　　Becalmed on the cold gray sea—
　　And chill mists lazily float
　　　All over my boat and me.

　　The breezes lie dead asleep—
　　　Not a breath in the idle sails!
　　And I wearily watch and weep,
　　　And listen for distant gales.

　　Shall I still drop useless tears,
　　　And sit here and wait and wait,
　　Till my head grows gray with years,
　　　For the wind that may come too late ?

　　To be idle is shame to the strong!
　　　I will lay my hand to the oar;—
　　And the craft that has waited long,
　　　Shall wait for the wind no more!

OCTOBER DAYS.

PUSH back the curtains and fling wide the
    door;
  Shut not away the light nor the sweet air,
Let the checked sunbeams play upon the
    floor,
  And on my head low-bowed, and on my
    hair.

Would I could sing, in words of melody,
  The hazy sweetness of this wondrous
    time!
Low would I pitch my voice: The song should
    be
  A soft, low chant, set to a dreamy rhyme.

No loud, high notes for tender days like
    these!
  No trumpet tones, no swelling words of
    pride,
Beneath these skies, so like dim summer seas,
  Where hazy ships of cloud at anchor ride.

At peace are earth and sky, while softly fall
  The brown leaves at my feet. A holy palm
Rests in a benediction over all.
  O silent peace! O days of silent calm!

And passion, like the winds, lies hushed and
    still;
  A throng of gentle thoughts, sweet, calm
    and pure,
Knock at my door and lightly cross the sill.
  Would that their feet might stay, their
    reign endure!

But storms will come. The haze upon the
    hills
  Will yield to blinding gusts of sleet and
    snow;
And, for this peace that all my being fills,
  The tides of battle shall surge to and fro.

Life is a struggle: and 'tis better so.
  Who treads its stormy steeps, its stony
    ways,
And breasts its wintry blasts, must battling
    go.
  And yet—it hath its Indian summer-days.

MAGIC STONES.

THREE oval stones, worn by the lapping wa-
    ters
  Of wide Lake Michigan.   As smooth are
    they
As if some lapidary's patient fingers
  Had wrought their polished disks of mot-
    tled gray.

Long I have kept them; and I well remem-
    ber
  When, where I picked them up.   A sum-
    mer's day
Drew near its close; the sunset glory
  Flooded the land and on the water lay.

But not alone the sunset's gold and crimson,
  The sparkling waves, the white sails mov-
    ing slow,
These stones recall.   Dear friends were there
    beside me,
  With faces radiant in the evening glow.

What happiness it was to talk and listen,
  To say with confidence the things we
    thought!
To look straight into eyes whose open shining
  Itself was speech, frank, full, concealing
    naught!

The city, with its restless, fevered pulses,
  Was near, yet not in hearing, not in sight.
No smoke of furnaces nor roar of traffic,
  Marred the still beauty of the evening light.

Alone, we few, beside the blue-green water,
  To us, for one brief hour, the world was
    not.
Its wild ambitions, and its throes of passion,
  Its fierce and selfish struggles all forgot.

And while we stood and talked, the glory
    faded,
  The shores grew dimmer in the failing
    light;
The shadows deepened and the lake grew
    darker,
  The white sails vanished in the gathering
    night.

'Twas years ago, and time hath wrought its
    changes;
  Yet have these magic stones the power to
    wake
A throbbing memory of friendly voices,
  Heard in the twilight, by the darkening
    lake.

RESCUE FOR THE PERISHING.

READ BEFORE A SESSION OF THE TEMPLE OF
HONOR IN JEFFERSON COUNTY, WIS.

Who hath the trembling hand,
  And eyes that are rheumy and red?
Who, amid darkness that knows no morn,
  Mourns over hopes that are dead?
  And who goes staggering by
  With weak and tottering feet,
With rags on his back, and cheeks aflame,
And hot lips foul with words of shame—
  The scoff of the pitiless street?

And who sits, sad and pale,
  Beside her desolate hearth—
A wailing babe on her patient knee,
  Sick and sad from its birth?
  While the heavy hours drag by,

Of what does this watcher think?
Why harks she so, as steps go past?
And why, when one step comes at last,
    Does she start, and shiver, and shrink?

    As one comes tottering in,
    With reeking and poisoned breath,
She well may fear, for she knows the work
    Of the fiery cup of death.
    More than my pen can paint,
    This sorrowful woman knows
Of want, of woes like mountains piled,
Of oaths, and curses, and ravings wild,
    And the weight of heavy blows.

    Reared in a delicate home,
    She remembers a happy time,
When the days were leaves of a pleasant
    book
    All written in dainty rhyme.
    She remembers peaceful nights,
    That were blessed with radiant dreams;
And rosy morns, and fleecy skies,
And the tender light in a mother's eyes—
    How long ago it seems!

    She remembers one day of joy,
    When she stood, a white-robed bride,
By the side of one who was more to her
    Than all the great world's pride.
    She stands beside him now,
    Pale with a mortal fear.
Her pinched, wan cheeks grow whiter yet,
Her great wild eyes are fixed and set
    On his face so marred and blear.

    It has come—that awful scourge,
    Whose terrors none can speak—
And the lips that cursed as he crossed the
    door,
    Now utter shriek on shriek.
    He sees   all fearful things!

A serpent crawls at his feet;
The dark panes glow with fierce green eyes,
And in yon dusky corner lies
    A corpse in a winding-sheet.

He feels on his shrinking cheek
    The flapping of goblin wings,
And over his flesh the slimy touch
    Of horrible creeping things.
    He writhes in the grip of fiends,
    That drag him down to hell.
Can aught redeem from a hell like this?
Could an angel's hand, an angel's kiss?
    Hark to the tale I tell.

There came to that dread abode—
    As come to many another—
Men of a tried and faithful band,
    Who look on man as a brother—
    Who look on man as a brother—
    However low he may sink;
Who stretch forth pitying hands to save
The fallen one from his self-dug grave,
    Though he stands at the very brink.

They came with soothing tones,
    With fuel, and food, and care;
And strong, brave words of cheerful hope,
    For the drunkard's dire despair.
    They bore him up in their arms,
    They plucked him out of the pit—
And now, in a home of calm content,
Where cheerful labor and rest are blent,
    Do peace and plenty sit.

The wife's wan cheeks grow red,
    And her smile is fair to see:
And a rosy boy, with golden hair,
    Climbs to his father's knee.

7

Brothers! such work as this
Deserves a laurel crown!
For the solemn joy such deeds must bring,
The loftiest genius, the proudest king,
Might well on his knees go down.

Oh, fathers with drunken sons!
Oh, sons with drunken sires!
Would that the bitter tears ye shed
Might quench these hellish fires!
Oh, people, grand and strong!
Arise in your kingly might.
Put from your midst the accursed thing:—
And the dove of peace, with brooding wing,
Shall on your homes alight.

BUBBLES.

I saw an urchin with a pipe of clay
  Held to his rosy lips; a rippling brook
Kissed his bare feet, then, singing, sped
    away.
  His cheek was dimpled, mirth was in his
    look.

The child was blowing bubbles.   One by one
  The tiny globes of rainbow, frail and fair,
Sailed upward, glittered in the morning sun,
  Trembled and swung upon the summer
    air;

Then one by one I saw them burst. Some
    fell
  Upon the stream that gurgled swiftly past,
Broke, and were gone forever. Balanced
    well,
  Some stayed a moment, but all burst at
    last.

I saw them vanish, and I sadly thought,
  With tear-wet eyelid and with quivering
    lip,
That such was history—thus frailly wrought,
  Men's lives are bubbles, Fortune blows the
    pipe.

A drop, a breath—no more—is place and
    power.
  The crowd that cries to-day, "Long live
    the King!"
To-morrow spurns its creature of an hour,
  And lays him low—a scorned and hated
    thing.

I see how men go up and men go down;
  I see the high and noble sink to shame;
I see the exile's ban succeed the crown;
  I see vile Slander dog the steps of Fame.

So must it be; the brightest bubbles burst;
  To grasp them is to clutch at empty air.
Is naught, then, certain? is all good accurst?
  Is this life all? Proclaim it, ye who dare!

God's Truth abides. We turn and veer
    about:
  We clasp our idols, and they fall to dust;
Our faith is weak—we plunge in seas of
    doubt—
  Yet there is still the Rock; and God is
    just.

DISCONTENT.

HEREIN is human nature most perverse:
  We spurn the gifts that lie about our door,
Tread on them in our scorn, and madly
    nurse
  A gnawing hunger that still cries for more.

And this for mortals all life's blessing mars,
  Turning to bitterness its offered sweet.
We climb up dizzy crags to grasp the stars,
  While unplucked roses bloom about our
    feet.

The stars are out of reach; the slippery
    steeps
  Prove treacherous footholds, and we trip
    and fall.
Crushed are the roses; disappointment
    weeps
  O'er bleeding bruises: and that ends it all.

We stretch out empty arms with longing
    sore,
  To clasp the mocking phantom of a dream:
We pant with thirst while standing on a
    shore
  Kissed by the ripples of a living stream.

From sweet, pure waters do we turn aside.
  Lured by false fountains in the desert gray:
We chase a vision o'er expanses wide.
  To find it grow more distant, day by day.

Why do we so? Could we but learn to take,
  With thankful hearts, the blessings at our
    hand.
To drink near springs, nor chase the phan-
    tom lake
  That swiftly vanishes along the sand!

Suppose we gain our quest; suppose we
    taste—
  Aye, even drink our fill, with lips afire—
Repentant leisure treads the heels of haste:
  In sad, remorseful tears ends fierce desire.

Life is too short to waste in vain pursuit
  Of swift delight that through the fingers
    slips,
Or, caught and held, oft proves a Dead Sea
    fruit,
  That turns to bitter ashes on the lips.

ON THE FARM.

How sweet to lean on Nature's arm,
And jog through life upon the farm!
Merchants and brokers spread and dash
A little while, then go to smash;
But we can keep from day to day,
The even tenor of our way.
(There go those horses! Quick, John! catch
    'em!
They'll break their necks! You didn't hitch
    'em!)

How clear and shrill the ploughboy's song,
As merrily he jogs along!
The playful breeze about him whirls,
And tosses wide his yellow curls.
His hands are brown, his cheeks are red—
An ever blooming flower bed.
Unspoiled by crowds, unvexed by care—
(Goodness, do hear the urchin swear!)

How soft the summer showers fall
On field and garden, cheering all;
How bright, in woods, the diamond sheen
Of rain-drops strung on threads of green—
Each oak a King, with jewelled crown.
(The wind has blown the haystack down!
I knew 'twould hail, it got so warm.
That fence is flat—my! what a storm!)

How soft the hazy summer night!
On dewy grass the moon's pale light
Rests dreamily. It falls in town,
On smoky roofs and pavements brown.
How tenderly, when night is gone,
Breaks o'er the fields the summer dawn!
How sweet and pure the scented morn—
(Get up! Old Molly's in the corn!)

Far from the city's dust and broil,
We women sing at household toil,

Nor scorn to work with hardened hands.
We laugh at fashion's bars and bands.
And on our cheeks wear Nature's rose—
(*That calf* is nibbling at my clothes!
Off she goes at double shuffle,
Chewing down my finest ruffle!)

We workers, in our loom of life,
Far from the city's din and strife,
Weave many a soft, poetic rose,
With patient hand, through warp of prose.
We love our labor more and more,
(John! here! *these pigs* are at the door!
They've burst the sty, and scaled the wall—
There goes my kettle, soap and all!)

HOURS OF PAIN.

WITH the hot blood rushing, swelling,
    Surging through my throbbing brain,
Worn and weary, past the telling,
    Nerveless in the grasp of pain,

Lean I on my thorny pillow,
    Strewn with torments o'er and o'er;
Every pulse a bursting billow,
    Breaking on a tortured shore.

But there come, in soft caressing,
    Gentle touches, loving hands;
As the soft rain drops its blessing
    On the scorched and thirsty lands.

Tender voices, softly falling,
    Drop their pity in my ear;
Sweet as tinkling waters, calling
    O'er a desert parched and sere.

Bless your music, sweet young voices—
    Dear young hands, you soft caress!
Pain is fierce, but love rejoices
    In its conquering tenderness.

OVER NIAGARA.

HEARKEN, friends, while I tell you—
 I will be as brief as I may—
How, while the drums were beating,
 And the great guns boomed away,
A pair of blithe young lovers
 Kept Independence Day.

I was passing the bridge up yonder,
 That crosses the creek, you know,
Near where it enters the river,
 That rolls with a mighty flow
Toward where the Cataract thunders
 Only three miles below.

I heard sweet peals of laughter
 Ring over the river wide,
And looked where a boat went tossing
 Out toward the rapid tide,
And saw that the prow was headed
 Toward the American side.

I watched the boy that was rowing,
 And the girl that sat in the stern,
And I saw that the two were lovers—
 It took but a glance to learn—
They were taking their trip of pleasure—
 Would they ever, ever return?

I saw that he rowed but badly,
 And my heart sank at the sight;
It is only the skilful oarsman,
 With a touch both firm and light,
That here rows across the river
 And ever returns at night.

I watched the frail craft tossing,
 In a tremor of dread suspense;
And I held my breath in the terror
 That swept over every sense,
As I saw that the boat was heading
 Outside of the "river fence."

They have passed it now! in the rapids,
  Where never a boat crossed o'er,
They are swinging nearer and nearer
  The Cataract's thundering roar.
They will never come back to the Queen's
    land,
  Nor reach the American shore!

There are flecks of foam on the water;
  There are white-caps on the tide;
And swifter, and ever swifter
  Down to their doom they glide.
Not thus in the joyful morning
  Did the youth think to wed his bride!

I hear the girl shriek wildly,
  As she points to the rocks before;
I see the boy's mad effort
  To turn the boat to the shore;
Then I watch him looking for something—
  Great God! he has dropped an oar!

My old knees they smote together;
  I could feel my cheeks grow pale,
As I heard above all the roaring,
  The sound of that maiden's wail;
And I clutched, as if *I* were drowning,
  My hands to the wooden rail.

Still I gazed, in my frozen terror,
  For I could not turn away;
And I saw them clinging together,
  As down in the boat they lay;
And the sight my midnight pillow
  Will haunt till my dying day.

I saw the boat swing over
  The crests of the first descent;
It was lost to sight for a moment
  Where the hollowed waters bent;
The next, on a rock, foam-covered,
  It poised, then downward went.

I saw no more; but others
  Standing beside the Fall,
Watching the beautiful rainbow
  That spans the eternal wall,
Beheld a few black fragments
  Of a boat—and that was all.

THE TOWER OF SILENCE.

HIGH on the cool, green summit of a hill
That crowns a foot-spur of the Western
    Ghauts,
There, stands a lonely tower. A grove of
    palms
Clusters about its foot, and far below
The warm waves lap the gorgeous tropic
    shore
Of rich Bombay. Strong, close-clamped iron
    bars,
Netted and intersected, crown its top,
And deep and dark beneath there sleeps a
    well.

This strange, weird thing—this high and si-
    lent tower,
That looks down on the city and the sea—
Is not a temple, nor a monument,
Nor yet is it a seat where telescopes
Are pointed skyward. 'Tis a common tomb!

Here, while the fetid flames of Hindoo pyres
Blaze on the plains below, and while the sea
Utters its solemn dirges by the shore,
The Parsees bring their dead. No graves are
    dug;
No cool, fresh turf, in its soft tenderness,
About the sleeper flings its garments green.
Here, high in air, beneath the solemn stars,
With faces smiling ghastly to the moon—

Now bathed in night-dews, now in noontide
    heats—
Lie in grim state the devotees of fire.
Glowing upon the reeking forms, the sun
Shines fiercely down—the god, before whose
    shrine
In life they bowed, in death are offered up.

But hungry ghouls swoop down upon the
    dead,   [share.
And, fiercely screaming, claim a ghastly
Vultures and eagles, every bird of prey
That haunts the crags of the wild Ghautian
    hills,
Here feed and fatten on the dreadful feast.
And when the sun, the dews and mountain
    winds,
Have ended the dread work the birds began,
When the slow-working fingers of decay
Have crumbled up the bleached and naked
    bones,
There is the well below; and, piece by piece,
They drop into its bosom, dark and deep;
This is the secret of the Silent Tower:—

Ajalee was a Parsee bride, beloved
And beautiful.   Her husband clung to her
With passionate devotion—yet she died.
So had he loved her, that the awful thought
Of giving up the form his arms had clasped
To the fierce talons of the screaming birds
Seemed horrible to him.   So, when he laid
His lovely sleeper on the Silent Tower
With a last kiss, love formed its skilful plan.
He built about her a close-netted screen,
At which the hungry claws might tear in
    vain;
Then left her to the moon and midnight stars;
To the soft washings of the tropic rain;
The mountain winds, and the sweet, sacred
    sun.

LAURA.

A VILLAGE street, a cottage-home,
  A Summer-night, a starry sky,
A moonlit porch where woodbine clomb,
  A sound of late feet hurrying by.

Two lovers, underneath the vines,
  With warm hands clasped, looked out on
    life—
A glowing scene, all sunny lines—
  No tears, no clouds, no stormy strife.

A sweet perspective stretched afar,
  With rippling streams and vales of green,
And Love the steady guiding-star;
  Could aught, could aught be thrust between?

How fair they were,—cheek pressed to cheek,
  Gold locks and brown in mingled strands,—
A fairer picture one might seek
  In vain through all Earth's sunny lands.

    *   *   *   *   *   *   *   *

The Summer waned; the nights grew chill;
  With stealthy fingers Autumn came,
And clad the copse and wooded hill
  In gorgeous garments, splashed with flame.

At eve, returning homeward late,
  Just as the frosty twilight fell,
I found young Laura at the gate,
  Counting the tolling of the bell.

The last stroke fell. Against her heart
  She pressed her hand. "'Tis he!" she said;
No other sign of present smart.
  Would she had moaned, or wept, or prayed!

    *   *   *   *   *   *   *   *

A grave upon a lone hill-side,
  Where Autumn leaves lay sere and dead.
Here oft, at the cold even-tide,
  Came silent Laura, bride unwed.

One morn they found her, still and cold,
  With white lips pressed against the stone,
While in her mantle's crease and fold,
  And on her hair, the hoar-frost shone.

United.   Round their lowly bed
  The fierce winds howl in wild delight.
Not thus, not thus they thought to wed;
  Not so they planned, that Summer-night.

NOVEMBER RAIN.

NOVEMBER rain!   November rain!
Fitfully beating the window-pane;
Creeping in pools across the street;
Clinging in slush to dainty feet;
Shrouding in black the sun at noon;
Wrapping a pall about the moon.

Out in the darkness, sobbing, sighing,
Yonder, where the dead are lying.
Over mounds with headstones gray,
And new ones made but yesterday—
Weeps the rain above the mould.
Weeps the night-rain, sad and cold.

The low wind wails—a voice of pain,
Fit to chime with the weeping rain.
Dirge-like, solemn, it sinks and swells,
Till I start and listen for tolling bells,
And let them toll—the summer fled,
Wild winds and rain bewail the dead.

And yet not dead.   A prophesy
Over wintry wastes comes down to me,
Strong, exultant, floating down
Over frozen fields and forests brown,
Clear and sweet it peals and swells,
Like New Year chimes from midnight bells.

It tells of a heart with life aglow,
Throbbing under the shrouding snow,

Beating, beating with pulses warm,
While roars above it the gusty storm.
Asleep—not dead—your grief is vain,
Wild, wailing winds, November rain.

TO MARY.

My heart is back in the past, to-night,
    As I sit in the twilight dim and pale;
The wide, brown prairie is vanished quite,
And another land steals on my sight,
    With wooded hill-top and sheltered vale.

Down in a hollow a village lies,
    With its peaceful dwellings white and
        brown;
And I see, as I scan it with loving eyes—
Save here and there some slight surprise—
    But little change in the dear old town.

Yet some dear faces I see not there—
    Faces of friends that I used to know—
Some that were dark and some that were fair.
I miss them sore, and I question where
    Are these that I loved, long, long ago.

Up on a hill-side, near the town,
    In a silent city, with portals low,
Under creeping grasses, now sere and brown,
Under soft, gray mosses, that long have
        grown,—
    Here lie some that I used to know.

And you—O friend whom I loved so well,
    Whom still I have loved, through all these
        years!
Your heart has bled, while a sorrowful knell
Slowly throbbed from the old church-bell,
    You have shed in your loneliness bitter
        tears.

And how fare you now? is life still sweet?
  When the sun set did the stars arise?
Are the paths made smooth for your willing
    feet?
Are you strong the allotted task to meet?
  Has the smile returned to your lips and
    eyes?

Would I could see you, and clasp your hand,
  And look in your face as I used to do!
But swollen rivers, mighty and grand,
And many and many a league of land,
  Between us lie, while I question you.

MY MOTHER'S WHEEL.

BROKEN, dismantled! would that it were
    mine;
  I would not keep it in that dusty nook,
Where tangled cobwebs cross and interwine,
  And old, grim spiders from their corners
    look.

From distaff, band, and polished rim, are
    hung
  The dusty meshes.   Black the spindle is,
Crooked, and rusty—a dead, silent tongue,
  That once made whirring music—there it
    lies.

Ah, dear to me is this forsaken thing!
  I gaze upon it, and my eyes grow dim;
For I can see my mother, hear her sing,
  As winds the shining thread, and whirls the
    rim.

So sweet she sang—her youngest on her
    knee—
  Now a low warble, now some grand old
    hymn,
Sublime, exultant, full of victory,
  Triumphant as the songs of seraphim.

Sweet toiler! through her life of crowded
    care,
  While grief came oft, and pain, and weari-
    ness,
Still swelled the anthem, still was breathed
    the prayer,
  Till Death came clasping with its cold ca-
    ress.

She sings no more; beside the chimney wide
  No more she spins. Years come and go;
Above her grave upon the lone hill-side,
  The snow-drifts lie, the summer grasses
    grow.

GOD KNOWS.

God only knows what fate the coming mor-
    row
  Holds in its close shut hand—
What wave of joy, what whelming tide of
    sorrow,
  May flood my heart's dry land.

But whether laughter, with its bounding bil-
    low,
  Rolls up in joyous swell,
Or sorrow darkly flows beneath the willow,
  I still will say, 'tis well.

And I will strew my seed upon the waters,—
  The sweet soil lies below,—
Whether with smiles or tears it little mat-
    ters,
  So it may spring and grow.

I know my hand may never reap its sowing;
  And yet some other may.
And I may never even see it growing—
  So short my little day!

Still must I sow. Though I may go forth
    weeping,
  I cannot, dare not stay.
God grant a harvest! though I may be sleep-
    ing
  Under the shadows gray.

I know not but the ruthless frosts may wither,
  The worms may eat my rose;
There may not be one flower or sheaf to
    gather.
  Blindly I wait—God knows.

FOURSCORE.

Sire with the silver hair,
Shrunken whose features are,
    Why dost thou weep?
Sad art thou, weary one,
Nearing the set of sun,
That thy work nobly done,
    Ends with a sleep!

Cheer thee; thy hands are worn,
Bleeding thy feet and torn;—
    Wouldst thou not rest?
On yonder Silent Shore
Soundeth no battle-roar;
There shall fierce storms no more
    Beat on thy breast.

Struggle and toil and care,
Sure thou hast borne thy share;
    Strength is but lent.
Young limbs are strong and free,
Young shoulders take from thee
Loads that weigh heavily:—
    Be thou content.

Under cool grasses sweet,
Creeping at head and feet,

Thus shalt thou sleep.
Under the autumn glow,
Under the winter snow,
Never a pang to know—
Why dost thou weep?

After the peaceful night
Cometh the fadeless light—
(Hope of the just).
After the sword and shield,
Palms shall the victor wield.
Count it, then, gain to yield
Dust unto dust.

TO THE MEMORY OF A YOUNG FRIEND.

SING a song with sorrow laden,
Sing a requiem sad and slow,
For the pure and gentle maiden
Lying with her head so low.
Loving was she, sweet and mild,
Half a woman, half a child.

Hands so helpful, past the telling.
Ah, how soon your work is done!
Feet so light, so fleet, so willing,
Ah, how soon your race is run!
Bright her morning rose, and yet
Ere its prime her sun is set.

In the great world's swelling surges—
Ceaseless strife of loss and gain—
Drowned are sorrow's mournful dirges,
Sobs of anguish, cries of pain.
Why for her such tears should flow,
Only we who loved her know.

Keen the wind that sweeps the prairie;
Keener yet the bitter breath
Blown from off the borders dreary
Of the silent realm of Death.

8

And we shiver—shrink with dread,
  As we cover up our dead.

Hard is parting—hard to sever
  Ties that bleed at every strand;
And the gap shall close, ah, never,
  In that broken household band.
Yet, while we perforce must weep,
  Sleep, O maiden! sweetly sleep.

O'er thee snows, descending lightly,
  Softly fold their ermine screen;
Choicest flowers shall blossom brightly;
  Grasses wave their banners green,
Summer breezes, stealing nigh,
  These shall breathe thy lullaby.

Tender is our common mother,
  Shielding from the storm and strife,
While Hope whispers of another,
  And a brighter, better life.
Even amid our blinding tears,
  Faith serene consoles and cheers.

A HOUSE-KEEPER'S QUESTIONS.

WHILE autumn tints fleck yonder wood,
  And lazy winds are sleeping,
I feel a speculative mood
  Come slowly o'er me creeping.
A strong desire within me stirs,
  To see some questions settled,
On which the great philosophers
  Have long and fiercely battled.
Calm reason now shall have its say,—
  (Dear me; my bread is burning;
And I am wanted right away,
  To see about that churning.)

I sit me down again to think,
  Commencing at creation.
I fain would follow, kink by kink,
  The long stretch of gradation.

But that's the trouble!—where to find
   The first stitch of beginning.
The tangled thread who can unwind
   To where commenced the spinning?
What laid that first primordial egg?
   From whence came life unending?
(Do, some one, answer this, I beg,
   While I—do up my mending.)

Philosophy, that swayed and bent,
   Through many a revolution,
Now, calmy settled, spreads its tent,
   And rests at Evolution.
But Doubt stands gravely at the door,
   And puts its puzzling queries.
This question asks (and many more):
   What *did* commence the series?
Did something out of nothing grow?—
   (That soup is boiling over!
On soup depends the peace of home—
   I'll just take off the cover.)

Things are; and on this world, we know,
   Dwells quite a population;
But how came mice and men to grow—
   I give up that equation.
Some other problems stagger me.
   Yon graceless scamp is growing
To just what he was born to be;
   His father set him going;
How far is he to blame if Fate
   Has botched his constitution?—
(There comes a beggar at the gate,
   And wants my contribution.)

Still other things I want to know:
   Why evil tongues are longest,
Why deeds of darkness prosper so;
   Why wicked men are strongest.
And why must life, e'en with the best,
   Be but a constant battle
With secret foes that never rest
   Until the last death rattle?

Why are the good so sore beset?
Why is man born a sinner?
(But there's a nearer question yet:
What I shall get for dinner?)

BEYOND THE RIVER.

The time must come, I know, when we shall
  part—
  All ties must sever;
This golden zone, enclasping heart to heart,
  Must snap and shiver.
But doth yon deep, dark stream, part ever-
  more?
Or shall we meet and greet on that far shore,
  Beyond the river?

If we shall meet—oh! would that I knew
  how!
  In saintly blessing?
Or shall we stand as we are standing now—
  Mutely caressing?
Is yonder life but this grown rich and grand?
Or is humanity left on the strand—
  Dropped in undressing?

Oh would I knew! The misty clouds that lie
  Those waters over
Still darkly droop, still mock my straining
  eye,
  Still thickly hover.
I call and question. Silence hath no tone.
In vain I ask how I shall meet mine own—
  As friend or lover.

Love is so precious, life so frail and fleet!
  Hearts bleed and quiver;
Tears wet the prints of dear departing feet,
  Gone hence forever.
Parting is bitter. If I could but know
That thou wilt be to me the same as now,
  Beyond the river!

Is love eternal? Still yon sullen cloud
    Answers me never.
In vain I plead; it folds its sable shroud,
    Silent forever.
But I shall know. 'Tis useless to contend
With shadows; yet all doubt shall have an ·
    end
    Beyond the river.

THE SOD HOUSE ON THE PRAIRIE.

A LOW sod house, a broad green prairie,
    And stately ranks of bannered corn;—
'Twas there I took my dark-eyed Mary,
    And there our darling boy was born.

The walls were low, the place was homely,
    But Mary sang from morn till night.
The place beneath her touch grew comely;
    Her cheerful presence made it bright.

Oh, life was sweet beyond all measure!
    No hour was dull, no day was long;
Each task was easy, toil was pleasure,
    For love and hope were fresh and strong.

How oft we sat at eve, foretelling
    The glories of that wide, new land!
And gayly planned our future dwelling—
    For low sod house, a mansion grand.

Alas! we little knew how fleeting
    The joy that falls to human lot.
While unseen hands were dirges beating,
    We smiled secure and heard them not.

One day Death came and took my Mary;
    Another, and the baby died.
And near the sod house on the prairie
    I laid my darlings side by side.

I could not stay. My heart was weary,
   And life a load too hard to bear.
That low sod house was dreary, dreary,
   For love and hope lay buried there.

DIED OF WANT.

TREAD lightly on the creaking floors;
    Speak softly—so;
With careful fingers ope and shut the doors;
Calk up that crack, through which the night
    rain pours;
    These rafters low
Bend o'er a traveller to unseen shores,
    Where all must go.

A scanty bed, a drear, unfurnished room;
    Dire noxious air,
Where pent-up Fever breathes its hot si-
    moom,
And Poverty has plied its brush and broom
    Till all is bare;
A pale, pinched face amid the midnight
    gloom,
    And damp, white hair.

'Tis the last chapter of a story old.
    One period more,
To finish all, and the sad tale is told.
Too late comes Charity, with generous gold
    And pity sore;
Too long since Famine and Disease and
    Cold
    Entered the door.

A glimmer of gray dawn through sleet and
    rain,
    That beat and beat
With icy hands upon the dingy pane.

Within, a solemn hush.   Fold smooth and
    plain
        The winding sheet.
But see! the poor lips wear a smile again,
        Serene and sweet.

Softly, good driver! scour not quite so fast
        The stony pave.
You know not how *your* final lot is cast;
Some dire disaster, some unlooked-for blast
        Or whelming wave,
May land you, like this poor old man, at
    last,
        In pauper's grave.

Replace the sod.   He sleeps on pillow low,
        Like other dead.
His deep and pulseless rest no dreams shall
    know—
No shivering pangs, though freezing winds
    may blow
        Across his bed.
But, softly fall, O rain, and winter snow,
        Above his head.

AT THE FALLS.

IN this deep solitude, amid the roar
    Of falling waters, and soft folds of spray,
I sit upon the green and sedgy shore—
    Sit silent, while the river rolls away.

What heed I here the hollow masquerade
    That men call life?   It surely heeds not me;
I am not missed from the gay cavalcade—
    None whisper, "This was *her* place, where
    is she?"

Little I reck! the page upon my knee
    Talks honestly, and yon white waterfall
Pours a deep voice of truth unceasingly,
    While the gay world is but a masquers' ball.

MY HICKORY TREE.

TOWERING close at my cottage-door,
  Tall and royal, and grand to see,
With broad arms reaching the greensward
    o'er—
  O, a mighty King is my hickory-tree!

Changing its guise with the changing scene,
  As the wheels of the year are onward
    rolled;
Clad all the Summer in deepest green,
  Now resplendent in robes of gold.

Here gather the earliest birds of Spring,
  When the Earth awakes from its frozen
    rest—
The tiny bluebird with sapphire wing,
  The robin sweet with its glowing breast.

When vines are green at the window-frame,
  The brown-thrush sings, and the dove coos
    low,
And the oriole comes like a flash of flame,
  And hangs its nest from the outmost bough.

On the velvet grass, in the grateful shade,
  The workmen lie as they rest at noon,
Cheered by the bird-songs overhead,
  Lulled by the honey-bee's drowsy tune.

And here, with friends, on summer-eves,
  We sit in the sunset's mellow glow—
Sit till the night-winds toss the leaves,
  And moonbeams sift to the sward below.

O happy scenes! But now no more
  We seek the shade; the wind blows cold;
The frost comes creeping about the door;
  The dead flowers rot on the sodden mould.

Splendid yet is my hickory-tree,
  As the gorgeous leaves come fluttering down
Like flakes of gold; but I soon shall see
  Only sightless heaps, all sere and brown.

Shook by the winds that go hurrying by,
  Down to the turf the ripe nuts fall;
And the boughs shall soon stretch toward
    the sky,
  Stripped of their nuts and leaves and all.

When deep drifts lie on the frozen farms,
  The naked giant, in scornful glee,
Shall toss in the storm his strong, bare arms—
  O, a mighty King is my hickory-tree!

DOWN STREAM.

I SEE a boat drift lightly by,
  The stream is wide, the current slow;
  No ripples break the sunbeam's glow;
Yet well I know that, ceaselessly,
  The great fall thunders down below.

I see the boatman idly lean,
  With listless hand upon his oar,
  Unheeding that the sunny shore,
With safe, still coves and banks of green,
  Recedes behind him more and more.

The sunlight gilds the golden hair
  That clusters round his stately head;
  A lurid flush, youth's rose instead,
Dyes rounded cheek and forehead fair,
  Caught from the wine cup's ruby-red.

I watch him, and I hold my breath!
  He seems like one wrapped in a dream;
  While swifter rolls the narrowed stream,
And, bending o'er yon gulf of death,
  I see the baleful iris gleam.

Why floats he so, like one asleep,
　While nearer sounds that awful roar?
　Awake, O friend! take up thine oar,
And stem the rapid's fatal sweep,
　Turn hither, hither, I implore.

I stretch my arms and loudly cry;
　I call until the welkin rings,
　At last he hears—the frail boat springs,
Trembles a moment doubtfully,
　Then slowly, surely landward swings.

Saved, saved at last! Adrip with spray,
　I see him stand upon the shore;
　And then my senses swim; the roar
Sounds like a murmur far away:—
　Would I might hear it never more!

HIGH AND LOW.

Down in the valley, a peaceful scene—
Streamlets winding through meadows green,
Rippling, smiling, their banks between.

Up on the heights, the torrents flash,
Rush and tumble, and roar and dash,
Seaming the soil with many a gash.

Down in the valley, the summer rain
Gently falls on the growing grain,
Softly taps at the window-pane.

Up on the heights, the tempests beat,
Hurling volleys of pelting sleet,
When winds and clouds like armies meet.

Down in the valley, through growing corn,
The warm wind steals, and the breeze of morn
Kisses the buds, and the flowers are born.

Up on the heights, the wind blows chill,
Smiting the heart with its icy thrill,
Shrieking at midnight sharp and shrill.

Down in the valley, a level street,
Shaded by trees whose branches meet,
Trodden lightly by tripping feet.

Up to the heights, the way is steep,
The stones are sharp, the chasms deep,
And oft the pilgrims pause to weep.

Down in the valley, a vine-wreathed cot,
A happy household, where strife is not,
Each content in a simple lot.

Up on the heights, one dwells apart,
A mark for many an envious dart,
Lofty, but lonely, and starved in heart.

Oh, would there were less of strife to gain,
With bleeding feet, with tug and strain,
Far, rocky heights, that are heights of pain.

The brightest wreaths of fame may rest
On throbbing brows, and royal vest
Oft has covered an aching breast.

MORNING VIEW OF LAKE MICHIGAN.

HERE on this rugged bluff I stand alone
And look out on the waters. Could I tell—
Which I cannot—all that I see and feel;
Could I but give the swelling thoughts a tone
That press up to my lips—a song so sweet,
So thrilling in its tuneful harmonies,
Should send out on the air its rhythmic beat,
That heedless wights should pause amid the
        street,
And listen with bowed heads and tearful eyes.

My eyes are wet. The beauty of the lake
At this still morning hour, draped in its veil
Of dreamy mist so soft, translucent, pale;
Its music, as the blue waves gently break,

Move me to tears. Yet am I all alone;
No sympathetic glances kindle mine,
No answering eye, where kindred feelings
    shine,
Another heart interprets to my own.

Ah well! Here are the softly gleaming waves,
Here are the gold-fringed clouds, above, below,
Which from yon heaven and from the waters
    glow;
Here is the sunshine, which my forehead
    laves,   [by;
And there the white-winged ships go sailing
The cool wind blows, and lightly lifts my hair.
Can there be solitude amid a scene so fair?
Can one be lonely with such company?

Behind me lies the city, fast asleep,
Save early workmen going to their toil
With sounding tread. The long day's dusty
    moil
Clanks not along the streets. The convent
    bell,
Whose tones above the dreamers softly swell,
Unheeded, troubles not their slumber deep.
The sleeping city and the pale blue lake,
The convent bell, the low waves' ceaseless
    break,
The morning mists—all these shall memory
    keep.

SPINNING TOW.

A LITTLE maid with braided hair
    Walks to and fro
Before a wheel. What does she there?
    The child is spinning tow.

In through the open window comes
    The scented breeze;
With drowsy wing the wild bee hums
    Out in the orchard trees.

The blue sky bends, the flowers are sweet,
  As children know;
Yet with deft hands and steady feet,
  This child keeps spinning tow.

Still works she; steady mounts the sun
  Through skies of May,—
The small task ends; the skein is spun;
  The girl bounds out to play.

She learns life's lesson young, you say?
  'Tis better so.
That life is toil as well as play,
  She learns here, spinning tow.

Years pass. Beside her own hearthstone
  A woman stands,
With steady eye and cheerful tone,
  Brave heart and willing hands.

This matron, who on household ways
  Glides to and fro,
Learned when a child, on soft spring days,
  Life's lesson—spinning tow.

INDIANA.

ON THE DEATH OF MRS. INDIANA DEMERRIT,
OF AZTALAN, WIS.

UNDERFOOT the grass is springing,
  All the earth is smiling sweet;
Overhead the birds are singing
  Joyful things each other greet;
While they lay thee down to rest
  With thy babe upon thy breast,
            Indiana.

Softly murmurs yonder river,
  Hazel-bordered, down the dell,
While, with mournful sob and quiver,
  Slowly, slowly, tolls the bell.

Voice of bird, or bell, or stream
　Shall nòt break thy peaceful dream,
　　　　　　　Indiana.

Aching hearts are throbbing, swelling,
　With a deep and heavy pain;
Breasts are heaving, tears are welling,
　Falling on the sod, like rain.
Sadly tolls the village bell—
　Tolls each aching heart as well,
　　　　　　　Indiana.

Quiet lives have most of beauty,
　Noiseless goodness most endears.
Mother-love and wifely duty
　Leave behind them saddest tears;
And the world can never know
　Why thy dear ones miss thee so,
　　　　　　　Indiana.

Drear the rooms that late did hold thee,
　Where thy footsteps went and came;
Arms are empty that did fold thee,
　Lips are white that spoke thy name.
Gone thy smile, thy gentle grace—
　Ah, thy home's an empty place,
　　　　　　　Indiana.

Where thy silent form reposes,
　Creeping mosses, eglantine,
Glossy vines and summer roses,
　Loving hands shall sadly twine.
Yet the fragrant blooms shall fall
　O'er a sweeter flower than all—
　　　　　　　Indiana.

Still and deep shall be thy slumber,
　Lying with thy head so low;
Naught shall fret, no care shall cumber,
　While the seasons come and go.
Fallen flower, with severed stem,
　Thus I sing thy requiem,
　　　　　　　Indiana.

EVERY DAY WORK.

GREAT deeds are trumpeted; loud bell's are
    rung,
  And men turn round to see
The high peaks echo to the peans sung
  O'er some great victory.
And yet great deeds are few. The mightiest
    men
Find opportunities but now and then.

Shall one sit idle through long days of peace,
  Waiting for walls to scale?
Or lie in port until some "Golden Fleece"
  Lures him to face the gale?
There's work enough; why idly, then, delay?
His work counts most who labors every day.

A torrent sweeps adown the mountain's brow,
  With foam and flash and roar.
Anon its strength is spent—where is it now?
  Its one short day is o'er.
But the clear stream that through the meadow
    flows,
All the long summer on its mission goes.

Better the steady flow; the torrent's dash
  Soon leaves its rent track dry.
The light we love is not a lightning flash
  From out a midnight sky.
But the sweet sunshine, whose unfailing ray,
From its calm throne of blue, lights every
    day.

The sweetest lives are those to duty wed—
  Whose deeds both great and small,
Are close-knit strands of one unbroken thread,
  Where love ennobles all.
The world may sound no trumpets, ring no
    bells—
The Book of Life the shining record tells.

BLACKBIRDS.

.DAY after day the blackbirds came
   And perched in flocks on my hickory-tree,
While the leaves, at first just touched with
    flame,
   Grew golden, then brown as brown could
    be.

And still they came in a sable shower—
   A flitting, chattering, noisy crowd—
And I wondered, watching them hour by
    hour,
   What they said when they talked so loud.

Sadly the leaves fell, one by one,
   Floating, fluttering slowly down—
Leaves so green in the summer sun,
   Now so withered, and sere, and brown.

The tree grew bare; I watched one day
   In vain—the blackbirds came no more;
And then I knew they had fled away,
   And my sorrowful thought this burden
    bore:

The winds shall blow through my hickory-
    tree,
   The sifting snow, and the sleety rain;
But, little I know what awaiteth me
   Ere the leaves and the blackbirds come
    again!

DOWN BELOW.

THEY say that under the ocean waves,
   At the feet of the rocks where ships go
    down,
There are halls of silence—peaceful caves,
   Where lie the sailors whom tempests drown,
Where monsters sleep, and mermaids fair
   Comb forever their pale green hair.

There is surf and foam when fierce winds
    blow,
  There is rush of billow and thunderous roar,
Still in those chambers down below,
  There is calm forever and evermore.
No wind, no wave; the sunk ship's mast
  Is out of the tempest's reach at last.

Life is a sea—so the poet says—
  And yet the deepest of human souls
Shows smoothest surface in stormiest days.
  Far underneath the wild tide rolls
Through hidden caverns in surging flow,
  As the gusts of the tempest come and go.

Underneath, perchance, a careless smile,
  The sorest heartache lies fathoms down;
And laughter is oft but a trick of guile
  To hide the pricks of a thorny crown,
In direst conflict no sound is heard,
  And the deepest grief hath never a word.

So, a great, strong soul—when truth is said—
  Is a sea whose heavings are out of sight;
It buries deepest its best loved dead,
  And sends out bravely its "song in the
    night."
There are throbs of anguish, terrible throes,
  Veiled by a surface of calm repose.

ONE HOUR.

ONLY to rest an hour! to loose the strain
  Of feverish toil—with quiet pulse to lie
And watch with folded hands the upper main,
  Where ships of soft, white cloud go floating
    by.

Neither to work nor think! to-morrow's care
  Folded and wrapped, and closely laid away;
To make no effort, just to drink the air,
  Whose warm, sweet kisses round my tem-
    ples play.
9

Some viewless sorrow may be stealing nigh;
  I will not weep for grief I do not know.
I will not shrink beneath this April sky,
  And shiver at the thought of April snow.

A bird sings yonder on a leafless tree;
  His songs are merry—would they be so gay
Did he sit pondering on storms to be—
  On sleety rain to come another day?

You tell me that the world is going wrong—
  What then? I cannot stay the surging tide;
Its many waters have a flow too strong;
  I cannot turn a stream so deep and wide.

Then let me rest; enough, just now, is *life;*
  Let labor and ambition wholly cease—
All loads laid down, hushed every thought of
    strife;
  For this one hour, I crave but perfect peace.

PROBABLY NOT.

My ships may come in from the sea,
  Laden with wealth untold,
And bringing it all to me—
  Spices, and pearls, and gold,
    In many a rich ingot—
    But—*probably not.*

The castles I build in Spain,
  That a breath so topples o'er,
And which daily I rear again,
  May stand, and fall no more—
    By destroying winds forgot—
    But—*probably not.*

I may find the shackles of care
  That fetter my aching wing,
While I long to cleave the air,
  And wildly to soar and sing,
    Lifted from off my lot—
    But—*probably not.*

The heights to which I aspire—
 I may reach them by and by;
And that which I most desire—
 I may clasp it before I die,
  With the longing and pain forgot—
  But—*probably not.*

I may find on life's battle field,
 Ere the going down of the sun,
A place to lay down my shield,
 With the struggle over and done—
  Some peaceful and sheltered spot—
  But—*probably not.*

I may find how, without any loss,
 I can lay my burdens down;
Some way to elude the cross,
 And yet to deserve the crown
  Which falls to the conqueror's lot—
  But—*probably not.*

HARVEST.

GREEN are the cornfields, the wheat is golden;
 Fresh are the footprints of radiant June;
Fair is the Earth, with all of its olden
 Noontide splendor, its midnight moon.

Night comes slowly, with soft hues blended,
 Purple of twilight and cloud-wrack dun;
Sounds and sights of the day are ended,
 Clatter of reaper and glare of sun.

Shocks of grain in the night show dimly,
 Dotting the swells of the prairie's breast;
Down where yon headlight goes gliding
  grimly,
 Courses the steed that knows no rest.

Whistle of engine, and jar and thunder,
 Startle the silence and then are gone;
Still as before, is the valley yonder,
 Softly as ever the stream flows on.

I think, as I sit here, idly dreaming—
   The wind on my temples, the dew on my
     hair,
And the radiant moonbeams o'er me stream-
   ing—
   Of another summer, as sweet and fair.

Then, as now, stood close together
   Clustering sheaves on fields new shorn:
Soft sweet winds of the summer weather
   Stole through the ranks of dark-green corn.

I think of a night—the moon shone brightly;
   I stood bare-browed at the garden gate—
I think of a hand on my head laid lightly,
   And a voice—to me 'twas the voice of fate.

     *   *   *   *   *   *   *   *

Life's sweet summer has bloomed and faded;
   Sheaves have followed the red June rose;
Flecks of frost in my locks are braided;
   Wait I now for the winter snows.

Yet, oh, yet, while life shall linger—
   Let its tides swell high, or ebb and fall—
Never shall ruthless, defacing finger
   Touch that picture on memory's wall.

OVER THE HILL.

WE met on the hillside—we both were
   young—
   Where countless thousands have met be-
   fore;
And read together the tender book
   That youth in all time cons o'er and o'er.

How sweet the rhymes! How brightly down
   Shone on our faces the golden morn!
Far up the path sweet roses clung,
   Soft blew the winds of the Summer born.

" Our path shall be one," he tenderly said,
"Up the hill, down the other side;
Whether heavy or light the burden be,
Only as one shall our strength be tried."

So we climbed together, young and strong—
For no toil is heavy to Love and Youth—
And plucked the flowers that fringed the
way—
Flowers that blossom for Trust and Truth.

How sweet the morn! How the hours sped!
And dancing beside us came little feet,
Sweet, tiny voices, and little hands,
Clinging softly, with clasping sweet.

Ah, the tender sadness with which one tells
Of joys that are dead! The morning gone,
Rough grew the way, and hard the toil,
As the weary heat of the noon came on.

And then he was stricken! falling down
In the rugged way, at the hot noontide;
And cold hands bore him away from me,
Over the stream to the other side.

O! weary, weary, the way I have trod!
The pattering feet beside my own
No more keep time, and the little hands
Clasp mine no more. Old, and alone!

I have passed the summit long ago—
Slowly, painfully, creeping down!
Gray locks are straying my temples o'er,
Where clustered brightly the curls of
brown.

At the foot of the hill rolls the sullen stream;
I am nearing it now, at the eventide;
I shall enter it when the sun goes down,
And meet my love on the other side!

A LITTLE LONGER.

A LITTLE longer the winds shall blow
   From the still white billows of frozen
     seas,—
   Shall shriek through the branches of naked
     trees,
And heap the valleys with hills of snow.

A little longer the land shall lie,
   Corpse-like, silent, wrapped in a shroud,
   While storms hold wake like a drunken
     crowd,
A fierce, wild rout—but the end is nigh.

A deathless heart in the frozen breast,
   Far out of reach of frost or storm,
   Throbs with a beat as soft and warm
As the pulse of a babe in its rosy rest.

A little longer the Winter-night—
   The silent sleeper shall wake at morn,—
   Shall wake and sing, with joy new-born,
Wreathed with violets, crowned with light.

Looking out over wastes of snow,
   Vast and boundless,—a realm of death,—
   We long for the South-wind's gentle breath,
For carol of birds, and for water's flow.

A little longer to feel the sting
   Of the creeping frost, and against the blast
   To close our doors and to bolt them fast—
Then to fling them wide at the touch of
     Spring!

O days of Sorrow! O Storms of Fate!
   Could we see the end, when clouds hang
     low,
   As we see the Spring through the Winter
     snow,
And know it would come—we well could wait!

LOVE.

FRET not if fateful bar
  Cause Love's delay,
Nor if some baleful star
  Cross Love alway.
Love crossed is better far
  Than Love's decay.

Love hidden in the breast
  Is hoarded gold;
By brooding thought caresst,
  It ne'er grows old.
Love satisfied, at rest,
  Oft waxes cold.

We pity those who part
  To meet no more;
We sorrow for the smart,
  The aching sore;
The joined, yet twain of heart,
  Need pity more.

Two sit at table, where
  Love once said grace;
A bond yet holds them there,
  Still face to face:
Love, jostled out by Care,
  Has fled the place.

There live whose wedding-day
  Was wreathed in gold;
Who saw time stretch away
  With joys untold:
Their lives creep on to-day,
  Gray, sad, and cold.

Love, set in daily groove,
  Drops its high mission.
The lives of thousands prove
  This hard condition:
The sorest test of Love
  Is Love's fruition.

O thou who through long years
   Hast dwelt alone,
Whose love, enshrined in tears,
   Holds secret throne,
This thought its comfort bears:
   'Tis still thine own.

Ye wedded who remain,
   (But ye are few)
Through all life's toil and pain,
   Warm, tender, true,
Earth holds, on hill or plain,
   None blest like you.

LABOR.

WELCOME, life's toil! I thank the gracious
   Giver
   Who finds my heart and hands their work
     to do;
That labor done still multiplies forever,
   And each swift hour and moment claims
     its due.

I pity him who sits him down repining,
   Bound in his idleness—a silken thong;
He hates the sun and wearies of its shining;
   His moments creep—for empty days are
     long.

My days are full, I have no far off "mission;"
   My work is near; 'tis only mine to stand
Accepting tasks that spring from my condi-
     tion—
   Doing, as best I may, the work at hand.

It may be small: yet, drop by drop is added
   To make the gentle flow, the steady stream;
The smallest needle, if 'tis often threaded
   By patient hand, may sew the longest seam.

The finest strands may twist into a cable;
  Small stones be piled till looms a pyramid,
Slow, patient thought may break a crust of
    fable,
  Beneath which golden mines of truth lie
    hid.

I cannot always see my cable growing;
  Nor always see my pile of stones increase;
Yet, while I toil—the still years swiftly go-
    ing—
  This fruit by labor bears; It bringeth peace.

THE FIRST BREATH OF SPRING.

THE drifts lie deep, the ice bound stream
  Wrestles in vain with its wedded chain;
The lake still sleeps, still dreams its dream,
  Under its bright, cold counterpane.

The woods are mute, save the mournful tune
  Sung by the wind in last year's leaves.
Still that cracked and dolorous tune
  Sobs and shudders and frets and grieves.

Winter is king:—yet, soft and sweet,
  Comes a whisper, a far, faint tone
Of distant music in muffled beat,
  Only a breath, yet it shakes his throne!

Only a breath! and so faint, so low,
  That I lean to listen, and bear my head—
Lean to listen—till over the snow
  Comes the sound of a velvet tread.

Who breathes so low? who comes apace.
  Treading softly, with feet unseen,
With muffled form, and with covered face?
  It is Spring that comes.—Long live the
    Queen!

Welcome! all hail to the reign so near!
  Thine hour is not yet come, we know;
We shall wait through days that are gray
    and drear,
  Through howling tempest and driving snow.

But we well can wait; the fields, the lake,
  Silent lie, like a realm of death;
Yet *thou* art near and the dead shall wake,
  We have heard thy voice, we have felt thy
    breath!

Haste, oh haste! In this hour of calm
  We have heard thee, but oh, to feel thy
    kiss!
Oh for the touch of thy lips of balm!
  And oh! to be drunk with thy draughts of
    bliss!

FAME.

THOU who canst rouse, by power of song,
    The heart of the throng,
See thou stir not its lowest deep.
Wake not chords that are best asleep,
    Lest echoes fell
Shall vex thine ear and affright thy soul,
Lest the praise which is blame—which shall
    work thee dole—
    Shall around thee swell.

Fame is like wine—a cup to sip
    With temperate lip.
Taste the sparkles that bead the rim,
It shall quicken the blood through brain and
    limb;
    But, drain it dry,
Thou shalt age in heart while young in years;
Thou shall learn what heartaches, sighs and
    tears
    In the bottom lie.

THE WAYSIDE TROUGH.

On the velvet hem of grasses green
  That borders the edge of the dusty way,
Under a maple's glossy screen,
  Is a rough-hewn trough, all battered and
  gray.

All through the Summer, wet or dry,
  With dripping crystal the brim o'erflows,
Pure as the rain that falls from the sky,
  Free as the air that comes and goes.

Into the trough falls a tiny stream—
  Steadily falls, both day and night —
In the noontide glow, in the moon's pale beam,
  Sparkling always—a thread of light.

This battered trough, and this tiny stream
  Are known for many and many a mile.
'Tis here that the wagoner rests his team;
  For this he waits—it is worth his while.

'Tis here that the footman, faint and sore,
  Lured by the streamlet's silver tone,
Rests till the midday heats are o'er,
  Then, cheered, refreshed, presses bravely
  on.

And children, loitering home from school,
  With hot, flushed faces and bare brown
  feet,
Dip their brows in the waters cool,
  With ringing shouts and with laughter
  sweet.

Whence does it come—this stream so bright,
  That falls in the trough by the dusty way—
This sparkling, musical thread of light,
  That tinkles and sings, by night and day?

●Back in the fields, at a meadow's edge,
  Under a bank, by trees o'erhung,
'Mid sweet-flag clumps and grassy sedge,
  Is born the stream with the silver tongue.

A deep, clear spring, with a household name—
  Through fiercest drouths it still o'erflows,
As pure and as cold as if it came
  From rifted bosoms of melting snows.

'Twas a dear old man (bless his memory!
  It should live forever, fresh and sweet!)
Who hewed the trough from a linden tree,
  And set it down by the dusty street.

He caught and harnessed the tiny stream;
  It filled the trough, and it fills it yet.
In the old man's heart was a simple dream
  Of blessing his kind—but men forget.

He sleeps on the hillside, peacefully,
  Whether zephyrs sigh or storm-winds
    blow—
The hands that hollowed the linden tree
  Were mutely folded, oh! long ago!

Still weary wayfarers stoop to drink,
  Where tinkles the stream like a silver bell.
Of the kind old man few ever think;
  But I know he would say—"It is just as
    well."

THE TALKING FIEND.

SAD is his fate, we may well suppose,
  To whose pillow at dead of night,
Comes a ghost in diaphanous clothes,
  And stands there, still and white.

It wouldn't be pleasant for you or me—
  The ghost that in silence stalks;—
But worse than a silent ghost can be,
  Is the fiend who always talks.

As to spiteful spirits, black or gray,
  If you keep your conscience clear,
And a horseshoe over the door, they say,
  Not one will venture near.

But there's nothing yet, as I've heard tell,
  That can lay this Thing of Evil.
Not saintly purity, charm or spell,
  Can banish the talking devil.

There are bolts and bars for midnight crime,
  Which in darkness prowls about;
But the thief who filches your precious time,
  There's nothing to keep him out.

Of all life's miseries dread and dire,
  Have sorrowful poets sung;
But worse than famine, or flood, or fire,
  Is the fiend with the ceaseless tongue.

You know him; he calls himself your friend;
  But your deadliest enemy,
Who presses hate to the bitter end,
  Is more of a friend than he.

Does he dwell with you? At your table sit?
  Then, pack your traps and fly!
Or be talked to death—and I've heard that "it
  Is a terrible death to die."

Should the fiend read this, he'll not look grim,
  But a smile shall his visage mellow.
He'll never dream it is meant for him,
  But he'll think of some other fellow.

FOREBODING.

I WILL not look for storms when skies are
    glowing,
  With hues of summer sunsets painted o'er;
When all my tides of life are softly flowing,
  I will not listen for the breakers' roar.

I will not search the future for its sorrows,
  Nor peer ahead for lions in the way,
I will not weep o'er possible to-morrows—
  Sufficient is the evil of to-day.

GRANDMOTHER.

Busy and quiet, and sweet and wise,
With a long life's thought in her gentle eyes—
    The hoarding of many a year—
Nearer drawing, from sun to sun,
To the peaceful goal of a race well run,
Writing her record of work well done
    In the hearts that hold her dear.

Grandmother's locks, all silvery white,
Seem to my fancy like bands of light,
    Crowning her sweet, pale face.
Grandmother's voice is tender and low;
And the fall of her footsteps soft and slow,
As hither and yonder, and to and fro,
    She glides with a saintly grace.

Grandmother's mission, for every day,
Is to do the duty that comes her way,
    Whatever that duty be.
To think of others, herself forget,
To dry sad eyes when her own are wet,
Is Grandmother's plan—and the best one
    yet,—
    'Twere a good one for you and me.

She has her griefs, though she hides them
    well,
Her heart still throbs when a tolling bell
    Utters its mournful tone.
For she thinks of a knell rung long ago,
Of a far-off grave underneath the snow,
And a silent sleeper on pillow low,
    Whose lips once pressed her own.

Thirty years—'tis a lonely while!
Yet Grandmother's face wears a peaceful
    smile
      As she sits in the sunset glow.
She is busy still, as the evening light
Falls on her hair, so silvery white:
And she softly speaks of the coming night—
      She is biding her time to go.

CARRIER'S ADDRESS.

MDLXXV.

HEARKEN, kind friends. Upon this New-
    Year's day,
    While hand grasps hand with warm and
    friendly grip,
    And joyful greetings leap from lip to lip,
Scorn not to hear the little I shall say;
    For, call it what you will—a speech or
    song,—
    I promise one thing: it shall not be long.

To hold before you the historic roll
    Of seventy-four, I don't pretend to try,
    (You know the record quite as well as I)
Nor yet to open up the sealed scroll
    Of seventy-five. I could not if I would,
    And, what is more, I would not if I could.

Evil, catastrophe, may loom ahead,
    Close-wrapped in shadows. What would
    be the gain,
    If one could strip them naked? Naught
    but pain.
We bear an evil twice which once we dread;
    And as to good, to be most full, complete,
    There must be some surprise to spice the
    sweet.

Some things have happened, and some others
     will,
     No doubt. I offer you these sage reflec-
          tions,
     Instead of going over the elections,
And wailing over past and future ill.
     The Old Year buried, vain regrets should
          cease,
     While welcome we the New with songs of .
          peace.

The world moves on; barred is the backward
     track
     With debris of the ages. Time sweeps
          by,—
     The months, the days, the moments,—noise-
          lessly;
And always, always onward, never back.
     Time hath no ebbs; its tides flow steadily,
     Ever, forever, toward a shoreless sea.

The past is buried; rake not up the sod
     For mouldering bones, nor water it with
          tears.
     Along with buried hopes let buried fears
Rest in the darkness.   Merciful the clod
     Which hides what it were pain to look
          upon—
     The "might have beens," the good deeds
          left undone.

Let the dead sleep. The present lives, we
     know;
     To grapple that is all.   None ever may
     Do aught of good or evil yesterday.
Its tale is told and ended—let it go.
     And, for to-morrow, not yet need we bear
     (Perchance we never need) its grief and
          care.

*   *   *   *   *   *   *   *   *   *

The days go by,—how swift their flying feet!
  The year just born will soon be old and
    gray,
  And down the swallowing past be swept
    away.
And this poor life—so dear, so frail and
  fleet—
  Is made but of such quickly vanished years,
  Ends with a pall, a grave, and mourners'
    tears.

The days go by; we cannot stay their flight,
  But he who fills them fullest as they fly,
  His year is longest—since 'tis measured by
What it contains. Four score were but a
    night,
  Lived in a dungeon; and scarce more it
    seems,
  Wasted in trifling, or in empty dreams.

LEAVE ME ALONE.

Leave me alone. I would not see thee more.
The storm is hushed, the agony is o'er.
    I would not feel again
    The passion and the pain.
Do not again come knocking at my door.

Leave me alone. Put not into my hand
A broken cup, though bound with golden
    band,
    Lest I with thirsty lip
    Once more its passion sip.
Still let it lie, all shattered on the sand.

Leave me alone. I followed, long ago,
Joy to its tomb, with tolling marches slow.
    Wake not my buried slain,
    Only to die again.
Leave me in peace—'tis all I hope to know.
  10

Leave me alone. I may not quite forget
The buried love, whose sweetness thrills me
    ·yet;
       But let the willow wave;
       Rake not a grass-grown grave;
Break not the turf, for fresh-wrung tears to
    wet.

CONFIDENCE.

Is it better never to hope, than to hope in
    vain ?
Is it better never to strive, lest we never at-
    tain ?
Is it better to cling to the shore and leave un-
    tried
Life's wide, deep sea, for dread of its storm
    and tide ?

Who ventures naught, he surely shall never
    win;
He naught shall finish, who never doth aught
    begin;
The sun may shine and the heaven may shed
    its rain,
But only the sower may harvest his golden
    grain.

To-morrow, we know, is dark with its misty
    veil;
The light on the path to-day is but dim and
    pale;
Blindly we grope our way—but 'tis better
    so—
What God hath hidden 'tis better we should
    not know.

Nobler and braver is he who stakes his all,
And takes his loss or gain as the chances fall,
Than he who folds his hands and idly waits,
Till the shadows gather darkly about his
    gates.

Shall we turn our ear away from a sweet refrain,
Lest the pleasant song may turn to a dirge of
  pain ?
Shall we close our eyes to the ray in the midnight gloom,
Lest it prove a lure that leads to the door of a
  tomb ?

Is it better never to love, lest love mistake ?
The passionate heart may quiver and ache
  and break—
Yet give us the warm, rich wine, though well
  we know
That dregs as bitter as death may lie below.

We sigh for the joys that were coming, and
  never came;
We sit in the dark and weep, with our hearts
  aflame;
We feel the crush and the grind of the silent
  mill—
Feel the crush and the grind, while our lips
  are still.

What, then! shall we spurn our life as a
  broken thing ?
Shall we fling a curse in the face of Heaven's
  King ?
Happy is he who keepeth his trust through
  all;
He may shrink and shiver, and falter, but
  shall not fall.

WOMAN'S WORK.

LET her not lift a feeble voice and cry,
  "What is my work ?" and fret at bars and
    bands,
While all about her life's plain duties lie,
  Waiting undone beneath her idle hands.

The noblest life oft hath, for warp and woof,
   Small, steady-running threads of daily
     care;
Where patient love, beneath some lowly
   roof,
   Its poem sweet is weaving unaware.

And soft and rich and rare the web shall be.
   O wife and mother, tender, brave and
     true,
Rejoice, be glad! and bend a thankful knee
   To God, who giveth thee thy work to do.

INDIAN SUMMER.

AGAIN the leaves come fluttering down,
   Slowly, silently, one by one—
Scarlet, and crimson, and gold, and brown,—
   Willing to fall, for their work is done.

And once again comes the dreamy haze,
   Draping the hills with its filmy blue,
And veiling the sun, whose tender rays
   With mellowed light come shimmering
     through.

Softly it rests on the sleeping lake—
   This filmy veil—and the distant shore,
Fringed with tangles of bush and brake,
   Shows a dim blue line and nothing more.

The winds are asleep, save now and then
   Some wandering breeze comes stealing by,
Softly rises, then sinks again,
   And dies away like an infant's sigh.

You feel the spell of these dreamy days
   I know—for your heart is in tune with
     mine.
You love the stillness, the tender haze;
   I know—for your thoughts with my own
     entwine.

But this dreamy calm, this solemn hush,
  The sleeping winds, and the mellow glow,
. Only foretell the tempest's rush,   .
  The icy blast, and the whirling snow.

We—you and I—must bow to the frost,
  When our locks are white with its hoary
    kiss;
Our last rose scattered, its petals lost,
  May our Indian Summer be calm—like this.

HAZARD.

A STRANGE and a wonderful thing is our mortal life!
Strange in its troubled joy, in its secret
  strife:
Strange in its helpless groping for hidden
  light,
With each step forward only a step in the
  night.

Hope is a siren that lures with deceitful
  smile,
Warbles bewitching strains with her lips of
  guile,
Sings of to-morrow's pleasure, to-morrow's
  gain;
But the gain oft proves but loss, and the
  pleasure pain.

Caught is many a foot in a silken snare;
Ploughed is many a heart by a golden share;
Many a harvest of pain is in pleasure sown,
Watered by secret tears and in silence
  mown.

A curse may lurk in the palm of a soft white
  hand;
Many a life is wrecked on a gleaming strand.

Fair is the Danger Isle, with her emerald
    shore;
But the ship that treads her rocks returns no
    more.

Fair is the sail that floats o'er a rippling sea;
Sweet is Love's thrilling strain, sung tenderly;
But dire the wreck that parts on the pitiless
    wave,
And sad the song that is sung at an open
    grave.

Bright is many a morn that soon clouds o'er;
Dark is the sullen noon with its angry roar;
Dark is the sullen noon, and the night is
    black,
And our stricken treasures lie in the light-
    ning's track.

Vainly we seek to pierce the dark Unknown;
Vainly implore of Silence an answering tone;
Vainly we ask of Fate her scroll to lend;
One thing only is sure—that Death is the end.

THE OLD STONE QUARRY.

GROWN with grass and with tangled weeds,
Where the blind-mole hides and the rabbit
    feeds,
And, unmolested, the serpent breeds.

Edged with underwood, newly grown,
Draped with the cloak that the years have
    thrown
Round the broken gaps in the jagged stone.

It was opened—I know not how long ago—
Opened, and left half-worked, and so
In this ragged hollow the rank weeds grow.

Why lies it idle—this beautiful stone?
Ho, for the pickaxe! One by one
Hew out these blocks—here is work undone.

There are possible towers in this serpents'
    den—
Possible homes for homeless men.
Who shall build them ? and where ? and
    when ?

Must they lie here still, unmarked, unsought—
Turrets and temples, uncarved, unwrought,
Till the end of time ? 'Tis a sorrowful
    thought !

All through the heats of the summer hours,
The wild bee hums in the unplucked flowers
That creep and bloom over unbuilt towers.

As I sit here, perched on the grass-grown
    wall,
Down to the hollow the brown leaves fall,
Little by little covering all.

So month after month, and year after year,
The rank weeds creep, and the leaves turn
    sere,
And a thicker mantle is weaving here.

And a day may come when the passer-by,
Threading the underwood, then grown high,
Shall see but a hollow, where dead leaves lie.

There are human souls that seem to me
Like this unwrought stone—for all you see—
Is a shapeless quarry of what might be,

Lying idle, and overgrown
With tangled weeds, like this beautiful
    stone—
Possible work left all undone,
Possible victories left unwon.

And that is a waste that is worse than this ;
Sharper the edge of the hidden abyss,
Deadlier serpents crawl and hiss.

And a day shall come when the desolate
    scene,
Though scanned by eyes that are close and
    keen,
Shall show no trace of its " might have been."

TRAILING CLOUDS.

THE trailing clouds hang low;
Their misty folds drag slow
    O'er the ground;
And the rain makes, as it falls
On the roofs and on the walls,
    Scarce a sound.

I sit and idly dream,
While the rain-drops drip and stream
    From the eaves;
And memory's folded book
Slowly opens, and I look
    Through the leaves.

I cannot see the town,
Nor the prairies, yellow-brown,
    Through the mist;
But these pages, blurred with years,
I can read them through my tears,
    When I list.

I see here as I look
Through the pages of the book,—
    Flinching not—
Gray shadows, glints of sun;
Lost battles, battles won;
    Woman's lot;

Green paths, with sunshine sweet;
Rough steeps, to aid my feet;
    Broken staves;
Love's rapture, wildly throbbing,
Then grief, as wildly sobbing
    Over graves.

Must ill all good alloy? .
Will sorrow, chasing joy,
    Never rest ?
Ah, why the bitter-sweet ?
And why the bleeding feet ?
    God knows best.

Listen!   A tolling bell
Sobs out its mournful knell
    Over there;
And I know that hearts are aching—
Perhaps some heart is breaking—
    Over there.

At last the clouds are lifted,
And sunset gold is sifted
    To the plain.
Oh, peace for those who grieve!
May it come like light at eve
    After rain.

WEIGHING THE WORLD.

I WEIGHED the world to-day—its golden treas-
    ure,
  Its gleam and glitter, all its splendid show,
Its pride, its fame—in most unstinted meas-
    ·ure—
  All its allurements that do tempt me so.

I put them in a balance, all together,
    Against one heart—but one, yet surely
    mine.
I wished for once to know for certain whether
    This way, or that way, would the scales in-
    cline.

Then slowly rose the piled-up, shining masses;
    As slowly, surely, did that one thing fall.
So have I weighed; and thus the verdict
    passes:
    I find that one true heart is worth them all.

www.ingramcontent.com/pod-product-compliance
Lightning Source LLC
Chambersburg PA
CBHW030903050726
47500CB00009B/990